What Readers Say . . .

■　■　■

". . . I couldn't put the book down. Alex and Jennalee posed soul-searching questions about God's faithfulness." L. H., Oregon

"Excellent book. Good information, great story line, cliff hanger!! Can't wait for the next one!!" K. P., Wyoming

". . . I love that Rosanne can address issues that can be controversial in a very clear and loving way. Love her transparency in sharing her own Christian Faith along with respecting the LDS Mormon faith . . . I can hardly wait for the next book!" E.F., Oregon

"You inform readers about Mormonism without disrespect to their religion." J. S., Colorado

"What a great book. It is true that it is a Christian love story, but it also stands on its own as a really interesting, easy-to-read piece of young adult fiction . . . Overall excellent book." B.R., Massachusetts

"For me, this was a cover-to-cover read! Excellent story of love, learning, and growing up." K. T., Utah

"This is a very well-written, easy to read and actually quite informative Christian love story . . . I liked it!" C. B., Florida

"More adventure and suspense make this one a page turner. I loved how she continued the side storyline of Jennalee's older brother Brent who just returned from his LDS missionary trip. I can't wait for the next book!!" J. S., Oregon

Believe in Love Series

■　　■　　■

A Gentile in Deseret
Book One

A Saint in the Eternal City
Book Two

For Time and Eternity
Book Three

For Time and Eternity

Rosanne Croft

"I want the whole Christ for my Savior, the whole Bible for my book, the whole church for my fellowship, and the whole world for my mission field." John Wesley

Published in the U. S.
By Blackcroft Publishing
Copyright 2018 by Rosanne Croft. All rights reserved.
ISBN-13: 978-1729759004
ISBN-10: 1729759009

Rosanne Croft, Mesa County, Colorado
Formatting by Polgarusstudio.com
Cover design by Lynnette Bonner.
Author photo by Ray Croft.

Printed in the U. S. A.

Dedication

■　■　■

To the brave people of
Poggioreale, Sicily, and
In memory of the victims
Of the 1968 Belice Earthquake

Disclaimer

■　■　■

For Time and Eternity, Book Three in the *Believe in Love* fictional series contains observations, personal anecdotes and memories, as well as years of research on The Church of Jesus Christ of Latter-day Saints. Names are randomly chosen, and any resemblance to living persons is purely coincidental. The fictional characters' thoughts and opinions are their own, not necessarily those of the author. All Biblical references are in the New International Version, except for Proverbs in final chapter, which is stated in the New American Standard Bible.

Books by Rosanne Croft

■ ■ ■

A Gentile in Deseret
Second Edition Published by
Blackcroft Publishing, 2016

A Saint in the Eternal City
Published by the Author, 2016

For Time and Eternity
Published by Blackcroft Publishing, 2018

Once Upon A Christmas, Shiloh Run Press;
An imprint of Barbour Publishing, Inc., 2015

Like a Bird Wanders,
OakTara Books, 2009

Chapter One
Forever Marked

Massimo's hollow breathing terrified Alex. Pneumonia ravished his cellmate's lung. He needed antibiotics! The only answer was to escape their prison. In desperation, he whittled at the jail door's frame with a brittle knife blade he'd found in the gravel.

Their *Camorra* mafia captors delivered food and water via a boy named Fuglio. Glancing at the nearly empty bucket, Alex hoped the boy would show up with more water. And food. His pants were loose around his waist. They'd taken his belt and given him a piece of string to hold them up.

With the last cup of water, he bathed Massimo's feverish head, using the blindfold he'd worn during his capture. How long ago was it? Ten days, the last two with Massimo.

He shuddered, remembering the road block and how he'd scrambled out of the Maserati before the crash flattened it. Such a beautiful car. If only he hadn't agreed to meet the Putifaros in Abruzzo that day, the gorgeous car would now be safely parked at his uncle's winery near Rome.

Alex remembered guns pointed at him, how they'd ordered him to drop his wallet on the ground. The mafia men came up behind him, poked guns into his back, and tied a blindfold tight around his eyes. Hours later, after a ride in the back of a van, they pushed him into a dank jail cell where he landed face-down on the gravel, tearing the knees of his thin suit pants.

The mafia probably wanted a ransom, but despite his fancy car, Uncle

Lucio *owed* more money than he had. Already a week in solitary, Alex was sure his uncle hadn't come up with the money. That's why he'd talked his captors into allowing him to care for Massimo. They'd escape together.

In his old cell, he explored a dark tunnel, and discovered a cache of forgotten wine. With one taste, he concluded it came from the vineyards around the village of Taurasi, in Campania. Knowing this, he pinpointed their position to a cell in one of the ancient Lombard castles that towered above the valleys of the region. He squeezed his eyes shut, trying to recall the map of Campania, so he'd know which direction to carry Massimo once they got out.

Possessing top sommelier skills was one thing, but now he wished he had the breakout ingenuity of Houdini. Massimo's cell door just wasn't easy to spring open. So, Alex continued to chisel off splinters of wood near the hinges of the half-rotted door. He vowed to use his waning strength to break free and find help.

Singing worship songs bolstered his courage, and calmed Massimo's feverish breathing. Hours later, when a pile of wood chips lay scattered around his feet, he shook his stiff legs and looked out the barred window. Where was that streetwise ragamuffin, Fuglio, with the water?

Strange. An eerie fireball pulsated in the sky with an electrical glow. Glowing in a curved arc, it whirled bright light far above the prison window. Hadn't he seen something like this, on a YouTube channel about weather? Alex stared at the phenomena, mesmerized as the bright aurora trembled. Static electricity crackled in the air around him.

A sudden rumble filled his ears, like a train bearing down on him. It was followed by a jolt and violent shaking. The dirt floor rocked under his beat-up dress shoes. Losing his balance, he fell next to Massimo, who woke up with eyes round and afraid.

"*Terremoto!*" Massimo said, though Alex could hardly hear him for the roar. *Earthquake.*

Somehow, he crawled back to the window and pulled himself up by grasping the bars. A tree on the edge of the rocky cliff swayed in impossible directions until it snapped in two, crashing down with no sound . . . any noise had been swallowed by the thunder of the earthquake.

He and Massimo had to get out. The wooden door under his fingers rattled and shook. Jumping away from it, he rushed at the door, kicking it with all he had. Nothing. Then, another sudden jolt sent splinters flying as the doorframe buckled to the ground along with Alex.

A door-shaped sky filled his view. They were free! Spitting dirt, he stood up, crouching like a surfer during another undulating tremor. When it died down, an eerie silence followed. He could hear blood rush through his ears.

"We're out of here!" he shouted, pulling Massimo into a fireman's carry position over his shoulder. Lucky for him, the young man was not as massive as his name implied, but thin and wiry.

Alex carried him outside, and staggered downhill to a grassy spot where Fuglio clung to a lone sapling, his face contorted in sheer terror. The boy had braced his feet wide above a heavy-looking bag. His thick hair, as always, stood straight upwards from his head making him look electrified.

"Fuglio!" Alex shouted. "Come with us! We'll find help."

The urchin blinked, and gazed at something in the sky. Suddenly, the soil liquefied under their feet as a strong aftershock threw him off his feet. Alex twisted and fell headfirst with Massimo tangled under his legs. Sudden pain and dazzling light struck his head. He shut his eyes.

When the hurt subsided, he forced his eyes open to look up at the thousand year-old castle they'd just escaped from. He watched the walls shudder and implode, punching out blasts of crushed rock. Everything seemed to happen in slow-motion. White dust rained down on him as his former prison plunged down the hillside, landing in a pile of foundation stones.

When the aftershock ended, not a sound could be heard, until in the distance, Alex heard sirens in the town below. His forehead felt wet.

Massimo pointed at the new ruin. "Your cell is gone. Mine? Still there." A coughing fit transformed his face to a gray color.

"I got into yours just in . . . t . . . time." He heard his words slur.

Alex sat up, squinting with pain and Massimo reached out and touched him. "Your head, Alessandro, it bleeds."

He wiped his temple with his hand, finding a wide-open wound. By instinct, he knew it needed stitches. Lots of them. But he said, "I'll be okay."

The boy was crying loudly and Alex got to his feet. Shaking slightly, he walked over to Fuglio, still clinging to the tree. After peeling tiny fingers off the sapling's trunk, Alex leaned over to pick him up in comfort, but the boy grabbed his pants leg instead and pointed to the bushes.

"*Motociclo!*" shouted Fuglio.

Alex saw a motorbike half hidden in the bushes. Now they could really get away! He went back for Massimo and gently positioned his limp body behind the driver's saddle. Fuglio, who let go of Alex to grab his bag, piled on in front. Then he got on, hoping the thing would run. It took a tense minute to start the rusty scooter. What a relief it was to hear it thrum into action.

Peering through the blood in his eyes, he never let up on the gas, weaving through pot holes once he found the road. Cool wind surrounded them, and he took a deep breath. They'd escaped, but would they find help? Racing on dirt roads and through fields with Fuglio pointing the way, they traversed down a hill and spotted black smoke rising from Taurasi half a kilometer away.

Orange flames surrounded a gas station, and smoke from it spread through the air, filling his nostrils with acrid fumes. Taurasi was a smoldering wreck but somehow, he had to find a hospital, a clinic, or anyone who could help.

Fuglio groaned as the scooter sputtered and died. The gas gauge showed *vuoto*, empty. There was no hope of getting any farther on this ride.

Massimo went into a coughing fit as they climbed off. "Leave me," he whispered, "I cannot walk that far."

"I'm not leaving you," Alex said, his speech no longer garbled. "I'll carry you."

He led them towards town, with Fuglio gripping his pant leg with one hand and dragging his bag with the other. Massimo slumped over Alex's shoulder like a limp sack. Cries and screams grew louder as they entered the edge of town and found the main street.

Disarray filled his line of sight. A window frame teetered on a pyramid of fallen brick. In the middle of the street, a photograph of a smiling family stared up at him, its shattered glass mixed with other broken panes.

Survivors dug at debris piles, staggering around, bewildered. Many clung to valued possessions as they hurried away.

Sadness overcame Alex as he heard church bells begin to sound from a lone steeple that was missing bricks like lost teeth. The bells rang out, begging for aid. His own surname, Campanaro, meant 'bell ringer', and he pictured himself pulling the ropes, swinging the iron carillon, hoping God himself would hear. *Help us, Jesus,* he prayed.

He and Fuglio walked against the flow of villagers pouring from the town. His head pounded. Just ahead, tiles slid off a roof and shattered on the street. A woman with ratty hair wandered through the ruins crying out a name over and over.

Fuglio waved his hands, and pointed to a Red Cross clinic. A crowd of survivors milled in front of the closed doors. Alex let Massimo down on his feet, supporting him with his left arm.

"The *Croce Rossa*," said Fuglio, "the *Signore* can get medicine for his noo . . . monya."

"Thanks to your uncle and his *Mafiosi* pals," said Alex, "this case of pneumonia's already ten days old."

Fuglio looked somber, his miniature Roman nose prominent on his face. "You also need help, *Signore*. Your head is very bad."

"Don't you know you're not supposed to tell the wounded how bad they look? Anyway, heads bleed a lot," Alex said, bluffing. He knew he needed stitches.

He was dizzy, but he couldn't stop now. If he quit, they'd lose hope. As he gazed at the mob trying to get into the Red Cross clinic, he knew finding antibiotics for a case of pneumococcal pneumonia might be impossible, even here. And how long could Massimo last without them?

Victims, some holding crying children, pushed forward as the clinic doors opened. Behind him, two weeping men held a blanket between them, and Alex saw a limp, white-faced girl inside. Death shrouded her, but Alex shouted, "*Fare spazio!*" anyway, motioning for the men to cut ahead of him.

At the same time, the door opened and a Red Cross nurse planted her body to block it, and begged the crowd in a loud voice to stay outside the building. She told them the two-story building would not be safe. Pandemonium erupted and the mob whirled around in a panic.

Alex, too, moved away fast, searching for a safe place to go. But first, he spotted a news reporter and cameraman beside the clinic, using it as a backdrop for a news report. A fuzzy thought came to him. If only he could move his little group behind the reporter, *someone* might see them on camera. Maybe Uncle Lucio, or . . . Jennalee.

Thinking about Jenn sparked a foggy photo in his brain; a memory of her sparkling blue eyes, and kissing the top of her head under the street lamp in Rome. It was the last time he'd seen her, and he ached to see her again. He would beg her forgiveness for letting his pride come between them.

Sidling over to where he thought the camera would catch his face, he looked full on at the lens, praying someone would recognize him or Massimo.

The reporter spoke in a British accent, announcing: "Italy's Prime Minister has declared a state of emergency for Taurasi, Italy, the epicenter of a 6.8 earthquake. The death toll stands at ninety-eight and is likely to rise. Fearing severe aftershocks, hundreds are on the streets or heading away from the destroyed town. This is Silvestro Icarino from the BBC, reporting at the Red Cross in Taurasi, Italy."

Did he say the British Broadcasting Company? The report would go worldwide, and maybe Mom or his brother, Gabe, would see it.

His shoes vibrated again beneath him. Another aftershock rumbled through the ground, and adrenaline rocketed to his head. This time it was a living dragon, with murderous intent to raze every stone still standing.

In his peripheral vision, the wall of the Red Cross clinic heaved in a weird motion. He froze, watching another building across the street get sucked down in a column of dust.

"*Andiamo!*" Fuglio shrieked, tugging on his pants.

The bold "*Let's go!*" snapped Alex back into action. He scooped up Massimo and they scrambled to the only open place, the center of the wide street.

Billows of gray dust swept by them, and the sound of bricks hitting pavement rattled Alex, but what happened next sickened him. The shaking noise stopped, except for a bizarre creaking sound followed by a few seconds of silence. Then Alex felt a thud through his feet and heard a crash as the two-story Red Cross building hit the ground. He twisted his neck around, in agony about what he'd see.

The medical clinic was no more, marked only by a pile of bricks and plaster. The crowd of people around it, the BBC reporter and his cameraman had all disappeared. Wailing villagers scrambled to the smoldering wreckage to try to dig out any of the living.

Fuglio gulped sobs. "They're . . . it's all gone," he said.

"But you . . . you saved us, Fuglio," said Alex. "You shouted 'Andiamo' just in time."

The boy took a deep breath and quit crying. They stood helpless before the horrendous scene. Alex's head throbbed again and he wiped more blood out of his eyes. When would this nightmare end?

He held Massimo tighter against his chest as the sick man clutched his neck. Massimo coughed for a full minute and a red spot of blood appeared on Alex's shirt. Alex repositioned the weak man with his arm. *If only help would come.*

Alex had no choice but to pick a careful path through zigzags of blacktop and concrete. They passed whining dogs digging in debris for their owners, as he led his little group out of the chaotic town.

A weak crying sound resounded in his ears. Alex spotted a baby wailing from its high chair in a second story blue-tiled kitchen, cut away like a broken dollhouse open to the world. He paused, summoning the energy to help. To his relief, a young man scrambled up the stairs to save the child. The baby's cries stopped as he plucked her from the high chair. Here was one good thing, then, a saved baby girl.

Supporting a man too weak to walk on his own, it took a long time for Alex to reach an abandoned vineyard sloping down a soft hill. Fuglio walked close beside him, with a less firm grip on his pant leg.

Harvest had begun, and grapes filled abandoned baskets. His eyes and taste buds recognized these Aglianico grapes, the round globes of rich juice you'd expect from this soil.

Massimo smiled. With a raspy voice, he asked, "Do you hear the music, Alessandro?"

"No, friend, you're hallucinating. What song do you hear?"

"It is the *aria* from Carmen. *Bella* . . ."

"Wish I could hear it, Massimo. A great *aria* in the midst of this mess." How would he ever be able to enjoy music like that again, and think that all was right in the world?

A vise seemed to close on his head. *Lord Jesus, you've got to help us.* His brain became so foggy, he couldn't think of what to do next. But he wouldn't give in to it; their survival depended on him. Nausea caused bile to rise in his throat and he had to punch it down along with his fear.

Massimo moaned. "I'm so tired. *Fratello*, there are colors dancing around your head." The poor guy's eyes looked glazed over. Was this a sign he was about to die?

"Colors? I see red," Alex said, "red blood, red grapes and a red sun. But here's a shady fig tree, let's rest here." Alex laid Massimo down, where he curled into a fetal position, his sweaty hair sticking to his head, making him appear like the too-late girl on the stretcher.

Chapter Two

Captives Freed

Watching TV news in a café in central Italy, Jennalee covered her mouth in horror. A knot formed in her throat.

Even with a ten-day beard, she easily recognized Alex's bloody face amongst the crowd behind the BBC reporter. He stared with intent into the lens, his wild curly hair outlined against the Red Cross building behind him. Supporting a thin man with his arm on one side, Alex's other hand soothed the head of a dirty boy clinging to his pant leg.

He was alive, and she'd found him.

Then the camera panned other buildings and Alex disappeared from view. Her eyes still glued to the TV screen focused on the exact place she'd seen him, she continued to watch. Dismayed, she saw the camera angle off as the reporter interviewed people around the clinic.

"Brent!" she shouted for her brother. He hurried to her side, holding a cream-topped Italian soda in his hand. "I saw Alex on the news report about the earthquake! He's in a place called Taurasi. And he's hurt, his head's bleeding."

"What? An earthquake? I didn't know."

Brent studied the TV screen with her, watching for any trace of Alex, but the report ended abruptly. A tall guy, he tried to reassure her by putting his arm around her shoulders. "At least we know where he is, and that he's alive."

Her quick mind raced ahead. "The mafia must've taken him there, but where is it?" Jennalee's voice wobbled. She strode over to the café's waiter and asked about the town of Taurasi.

"*Si*," he said, "it is south from this region, near Naples, three hours by car. A terrible earthquake there. Excuse, *Signorina*, did you see the headline under the BBC report?"

She shook her head.

"The *Croce Rosso* fell and killed the BBC reporter and his cameraman." He shook his head sadly. "You did not know him, did you?"

The air left her lungs. After a week of searching, by incredible chance, she'd found Alex, bleeding but alive. Now, to find out the building behind him had fallen . . . no, this could not happen! She'd choose to believe that God determined this coincidence and trust that Alex *hadn't* been crushed, that he was alive and could be found.

Brent led her back to the table they'd been sitting at, as a soccer game recommenced on the TV.

Jennalee watched it a second before her anger erupted. "How can they put a game on after what happened?"

"Are you okay, Jenn?" asked Brent. "Want some water or something?"

She grabbed his arm. "We have to go look for him. Now."

"Jenn . . . Taurasi's hours away, over snowy mountains, in the province of Avellino," Brent said, looking at a map on his cell phone. "And who knows if the roads are passable? We have nothing but a scooter."

"We're going there, Brent." Lifting her chin, she stared down her older brother. "Alex looked into the camera on purpose. God wouldn't let us get this far to find him dead, would he?" She could barely hear her own voice as hot tears began to flow.

Alex was alive, he had to be.

Brent wrinkled his brow. "I'll call Alex's Uncle Lucio. He planned to drive here from Rome tomorrow. We'll go in his car."

"No, we're going *now*. He can meet us after we find Alex."

Brent sighed. "Somehow, I knew this would happen."

"Alex has hit his head, and the man and boy with him aren't in good shape either." She willed herself to stop crying, while her brother argued.

"Listen, the reality is we only have a motorbike, Jenn. It's going to be cold on the highway. Not to mention dark by the time we get there."

Her exasperation with Brent swelled. "Motorbikes can go where cars can't. It's just three hours from here, isn't it?"

Brent shook his head. "Try five. Up a couple of mountain passes to a town where there's been a major earthquake. Think no electricity, roadblocks, chunks of concrete, landslides. We'll go, Jenn, but that's what we're up against."

She clamped her mouth shut. They walked outside into the cobblestoned village square where Brent repacked his backpack on the scooter. Jennalee sat on the edge of the central fountain, and set her eyes on a bird splashing in a puddle inside the winter-dry fountain. Some brown leaves whirled up, blowing in a circle. She took in the crisp air.

Was it just a week ago that she'd run away from the strict confines of her Latter-day Saint mission? Her previous self would never have done such a thing. Jennalee had always considered duty, loyalty, and parental approval above all else.

But that was in the past, before Alex. Once she'd discovered he'd been kidnapped, she *had* to find him. Wouldn't any woman truly in love have done the same? And it wasn't just about her love for Alex. Now she loved Alex's Jesus, too.

The reality of Alex's faith had scared her at first. As a child, she'd learned the world outside the LDS Church could not be trusted. Now it startled her; she'd run away from a familiar life, a planned life, and everything turned upside down.

But it was worth it. Her own religious roots only skimmed the surface of the Bible's depths, and even though the words at the LDS Church might sound the same as Alex's, his words were backed by a liveliness of Spirit she'd never encountered.

She'd learned how deep a person could go to *know* Jesus. Her resolve to go deeper strengthened when Brent was sent to find her, and their long talks revealed how Brent's experience had been almost the same as hers. What a relief to know they were in this together, learning more about God's only begotten, not-made Son.

She zipped up her jacket, and her neck chain got stuck. Pulling the necklace out from under her shirt, she relished the sight of Alex's diamond and ruby engagement ring. A strong feeling arose in her. *Time to wear it.*

On the same chain was the cross he'd given her at their first Christmas together. Never again would she be afraid to show her allegiance to the Jesus who'd shown her his amazing love. Never again would she bury these gifts under her clothes. She put the ring on her finger, and arranged the cross to hang outside her jacket.

Brent came out of the café with some sandwiches. He bent low, stuffing them in his bag, and Jennalee put her hand out to stop him.

"Don't smash the bread," she said.

Brent gave a whistle when he saw her hand. "An engagement ring?"

"Right, but I didn't say 'Yes' at the time. Alex wanted me to leave my mission to get married, and at the time, I couldn't. Then he went missing, and I didn't think twice about leaving. As soon as . . . we find him, I'll tell him my answer."

"Don't worry, Jenn, a smart guy like Alex is a survivor." His eyebrows went up in a question. "Is it the same story with the cross around your neck?"

She swallowed hard. "A gift from Alex, out for everyone to see."

"Oh my heck, Mom and Dad are going to freak."

"I know. Half the Utah relatives will flip out." She shrugged. "But they won't change my mind. When I find Alex, I'm never letting him go again."

"First, we've got to find the fiancé who doesn't know he's a fiancé."

"Complicated, huh?"

Brent heaved a sigh. "We should at least call Uncle Lucio to tell him we know where Alex is. I wonder if he feels a teeny bit responsible for getting Alex captured by the mafia in the first place."

"C'mon, Brent," said Jennalee. "Uncle Lucio is the nicest guy ever. How could he have known the mafia ran the wine business in Abruzzo?"

"He's lived in Italy his whole life, that's how. Just saying."

"You can't be serious."

"Did you notice? He grins when he's nervous. Never trust a nervous smiler." Her brother threw in a grin of his own.

"You're wrong, Brent. Lucio is just clueless sometimes. But we can tell him we're going. And this time, we'll find Alex."

"Okay, your Italian's good, you call him. First, though, I've got to call Mom. She expects us to check in every day."

He punched the number and Jennalee winced when she heard her father's stern voice on the recorded message of their landline in Kaysville. She'd forgotten how it felt to be under his roof and his thumb, but at the same time, she sorely missed her parents.

Brent recorded a peppy message that everything was fine, and they'd be returning home after they'd seen more of Italy. Afterwards, he looked at her sideways. "Something's weird at home, Jenn."

"What do you mean?"

"It's Mom. She's not picking up again. After I got home, there were heated *discussions* behind closed doors. Then, after you ran away from your mission . . . Mom sent me to find you, and I don't know. . . Dad's always gone."

"I'm sure it's business."

"He definitely has business in Las Vegas, but what kind?" Brent looked deep in thought, and then brightened up. "Hey, I've got an idea," he said. "Just a sec, I need to make another call."

She saw a picture of a pretty young woman before he said, "Hello, Rachel?" into the phone. It was the evangelical Christian girl he'd met in Argentina.

Shrugging, she went inside to find a restroom, and when she came out, Brent's face beamed with joy.

"What did your Rachel say? Isn't she here in Italy on a church mission?"

"Right. I just called to ask for prayer, but you'll never guess. At this very moment, she's in a 'Youth with a Mission' van going to the epicenter to help. If we're fast, they'll meet us in Castel di Sangro where the road splits. We can ride with them."

Relieved, she said, "Wow, let's hurry. But didn't they have to get permission? If you ask me, that's a loosely structured mission. Not like ours."

Brent put on his jacket. "I don't get it either, but I know one thing:

13

Rachel's a missionary for Jesus and the Word, not any church or religion."

"Funny how we *thought* our mission was for Jesus Christ. We thought we had the absolute truth in the LDS faith."

"We were told that all our lives. But deep down, did you ever feel there might be something not right about our religious beliefs?"

"Sometimes," said Jennalee, "but I never truly understood until Alex helped me compare." She climbed on the back of the scooter. Brent had purchased it for way-too-many American dollars the week before. "*Andiamo*. Let's go!"

The motorbike took off with a bang of smelly exhaust, and climbed the mountainous spine of Italy, twisting higher through dappled shade and evergreen trees. For once she was glad of her warm LDS undergarments. She adjusted her helmet and crouched behind her brother to avoid the cold rush of balsam-scented air. She texted Alex's uncle about where they were going, and then, with the noise of the bike covering for her, she prayed out loud.

In ninety minutes, Brent took an exit off the road where a bridge arced above an icy river and a modern hotel rose against a backdrop of blue and white mountains. With a homesick pang, she thought of the Wasatch Front in Utah, the formidable wall of mountains encircling the Salt Lake Valley.

They stopped, parking close to the entrance.

"Nothing like the Rockies, are they?" Brent said, holding his arms tight against his chest.

She shivered. "No, they look older, softer, like they've seen everything this world has to offer and they're tired of it."

Brent took off his helmet. "No wonder. They've seen wars and religions and fads all come and go for thousands of years. America is young and naive in comparison."

"Like the all-American LDS religion started a mere one hundred and ninety years ago?"

"That's exactly it. What a drop in the bucket of time! I can't see how it would stand up to the ancient moorings of the Bible and the archaeological evidence here and in Israel."

"I agree, but we'll talk about it later. I'm freezing, let's go inside. I hope they're here."

Like many of the ski lodges in Utah, the spacious lobby with its roaring fireplace led to a windowed restaurant. Memories of Christmastime ski vacations with her family stung her mind. Would they ever have those times again?

She asked the desk clerk if any Americans had arrived.

"Your *Americanos* are here, *Signorina*," said the mustachioed clerk, winking at her, "they leave a message for you to join them in the *ristorante*."

She had to smile when she saw Brent smoothing his hair with his palms.

"Don't want helmet hair. I haven't seen Rachel for a long time," he said, entering the restaurant where the smell of brick oven pizza assailed them.

A stunning girl with auburn French-braided hair bolted towards them.

"Hello, Elder . . .," she said, "I mean, Brent. I'd know you anywhere." She gave him an affectionate one-armed hug.

"And you're Jennalee," Rachel said, offering her a hug, too. "Happy to finally meet you."

Jennalee watched her brother's eyes resting long on Rachel's face. He'd been out with many gorgeous women in the past, but this time, it was clear he was smitten with this Bible-believer.

"We've ordered the best pizza in the world, and you've got to help us eat it," said Rachel, leading them to a table.

An older man, past forty, stood up and shook hands with them. "I'm Jerry, and this is my wife Judy." Judy nodded with a kind smile.

So, it wasn't just *youth* with a mission.

His wife said, "Help yourselves. We're finished, so we'll be outside making a few calls."

Cold and hungry, Jennalee had to fight frustration as the pace to find Alex slowed. Sighing, she sat down. After all, who knew when she'd eat next?

"No more for me," Rachel said, sitting next to Brent in the booth seat. "I'm stuffed."

Brent grabbed a slice of Napolitano pizza with basil leaves and mushrooms. "My first slice of the real thing. Or did I have some in Rome?"

"You did," Jennalee said, "don't you remember?" Though she didn't feel like eating, she took a piece, too.

Jennalee was struck by Rachel's clear, bright eyes as she talked.

"Brent missed you during his mission in Argentina," Rachel said. "He told me a lot about you."

Jennalee gave her brother a loving glance. "I missed him, too. Brent and I are pretty tight."

"So you came to Italy on an LDS mission?"

"Yes, then I left it to find Alex. Did Brent tell you our story?"

"Some, but texts and calls are nothing like a face-to-face chat." Rachel smiled.

Jennalee reached for a napkin and told her about meeting Alex, and coming to Italy, and finding him again. "Make no mistake, I still have respect for my heritage. But when Jesus says, 'Come, follow me', we had to, didn't we, Brent?"

Her brother gave her a smile, but a lump rose in her throat, a feeling of both grief and happiness. The possible loss of their family loomed before them, but somehow, she had joy because of the big God she'd found out about.

Rachel spoke softly, "I know Brent went through a lot when he went home radically changed."

"But your prayer texts helped me, Rachel," said Brent. "I still feel terrible about disappointing my parents, but I won't go back on what I know to be true."

"Me, neither," said Jennalee. "Eventually, I'll have to face the LDS authorities, but now I'm focused on finding Alex. We looked everywhere in Abruzzo for him, waiting for the mafia to ask for ransom until. . ." Her voice quivered. "Until I saw him on TV today."

"No wonder we got scriptures about setting captives free!" said Rachel.

Brent inclined his head. "You 'got' scriptures?"

"At our early prayer group this morning, before the quake happened, someone had a strong impression to read Isaiah 42, about God releasing captives from prison. So we prayed, and when we heard about the earthquake, we knew we had to help."

Jennalee recovered her voice. "Alex *was* freed somehow. But we've got to hurry. He's hurt."

Rachel's passionate voice turned up a notch. "We'll find him. Finished, Brent? It's all paid for, so we can go."

Outside, they found the YWAM couple waiting in a van piled high with supplies. Judy said, "We've been praying for God to tell us which road will get us there the fastest."

Did these people pray about everything? And did God always answer?

Chapter Three

The Winepress

Refugees in noisy chaos passed the fig tree where Alex guarded a prone Massimo. Women carried sobbing children and old men trudged downhill, trying not to fall. Scooters roared by, piled with people, throwing up dirt clods. If only their motorbike hadn't run out of gas.

Fuglio looked up at Alex, his face blackened with soot. "You still bleed, *Signore*."

"It's stopping. I'll be okay." Alex held the boy's chin and peered at his eyes. "Hey, under all that dirt, your eye looks black as grapes." He wondered why he hadn't noticed before.

The boy jerked his head away. "*Non e niente.*"

"Don't say it's nothing. Someone hit you, didn't they?"

Fuglio stonewalled.

Alex gentled his tone. "I have a feeling I know who. But you can tell me later when I can do something about it."

They'd been sitting on the ground, watching the late afternoon sun inch down. Alex clutched his knees, holding together the shreds of his dress pants. He'd have to buy a new suit. It was time to give up his high-class job and go back to Utah. Jennalee wouldn't be there, she'd still be on her mission, but he could wait for her to finish.

"We will die here, *Signore*," Fuglio said, his chin shaking. "No help comes."

"Not going to happen. Help *has* to come this way; the other roads are destroyed."

A small group of people camped around them, lying under the grape vines, too exhausted or injured to get far. Alex closed his eyes and laid his head next to Massimo, hoping it wouldn't be a cold night. Fuglio sat next to him, ever watchful.

Maybe it was his throbbing head, but he sensed a strange calm like being in an eye of a storm. He'd had the same impression before the earthquake hit, with weird lights outside his jail window.

"Do you remember seeing those lights, Fuglio, up in the sky before the earthquake? I finally figured out what they were."

"I remember. They were *angeli*, with swords."

"You saw angels with swords?"

The gaunt boy shook his head up and down, his eyes wide around his too-big nose.

"I believe you," said Alex, feeling too tired to talk much. "Science can't explain earthquake lights. And you know what you saw." Wasn't there something in the Bible about children being closer to heavenly things?

Alex took a deep breath. "I wish I had the energy to go back into Taurasi to find antibiotics for Massimo. But I'm worn out." He felt like he could sleep for a week.

"You can't go, it's all gone," said Fuglio. "My mother take me to the *Croce Rossa* clinic many times for medicine and now it is gone."

Alex never pictured Fuglio having a mother; he was like a weed sprung from the hardened cobblestones of Naples. But as tough as the little waif had seemed before, now he'd morphed back into a seven year-old.

Alex sat up and took him gently by the shoulders. "Do you know where your mother is, Fuglio?"

"I never see her after my uncle take me away to work for him." The boy held his lips tight.

Alex tried another tack to find out more about Fuglio. "We've been through a lot together, haven't we? You trust me? More than your uncle?"

"*Si, Signore.*" He sounded more like his impish self. "This morning my uncle says to take you food. He go to Naples to do . . . a job." His eyes rounded.

"What kind of job?"

He twisted away from Alex and stood up. "A job! To *do* a job!" the boy shouted, his hands jerking in the air.

"Okay, okay. I know mafia talk. Fuglio, it's not your fault your uncle's a killer for gangsters. He has to do whatever the head guy, *Signore* Casalesi, says."

Fuglio shook his head forward as a hiccup escaped. "He always leave me." *Yeah, after giving you a black eye.*

"Life's not supposed to be like this, Fuglio. Do you know where your father is?"

"I never have a father." Fuglio shrugged, his hands still in the air. "I stay here with you. No go back to my uncle. Never, never."

Alex couldn't hide his repulsion at the thought of men who used little boys as pawns in their evil schemes. "After we get Massimo taken care of, we'll find your mother."

Nodding, the boy rubbed his eyes with a forceful swipe. "I think she died. And if you die, *Signore*, I will have no one."

The tension crumpled the boy's face like a stricken building, and Alex hugged the skinny ribcage shaking with sobs.

"Fuglio, we're not going to die! God didn't get us out of jail to leave us here, stranded. You saw angels with swords, didn't you? What do you think they do? They fight for us!" Just saying it made Alex feel stronger.

Fuglio stared hard at him.

"Pray, *Signore*." The ragamuffin folded his hands.

"Last time you heard me pray . . . you told me God didn't hear me."

The boy whispered. "Did you pray to get away from *Camorra's* jail?"

"I did."

"I change my mind. God listens to you."

Alex laughed, his hand shooting up to his head. "Ooh, that hurts. Have you got some water in that bag of yours?"

Fuglio's face lit up, a mischievous sparkle returning. Wrinkling his long nose, he put his arm inside the cloth bag. In a flash, he brought out two rustic loaves of bread, a block of cheese, and four bottles of water. He handed one to Alex, who guzzled it down.

"You're a hero, Fuglio. That bag was heavy, and you brought it anyway. What else have you got in there?"

The boy rooted around inside the sack, and pulled out a red cell phone.

Alex stared. "That's *my* phone!" The last time he'd seen it was at the swank villa outside Rome, as he escaped the flirtatious Caprice Putifaro.

An association formed in his mind. "Hey, Fuglio . . . I know where I first saw you! You were hiding out in the Putifaro's courtyard, weren't you? Okay, how'd you get my phone?"

"I steal it." Fuglio leaned his head to one side, chin out, teasing Alex with the phone. Then, he laid it on top of his palm and held it out. Alex had to laugh again. The miniature mafia man imitated Alex himself when he'd bribed the boy with a pair of sunglasses to get inside Massimo's prison cell. Alex snatched it in one quick motion.

"C'mon, c'mon. Turn on. . ." he said, depressing the on/off button. In the dim light, it flashed Jennalee's picture and an icon showed an empty battery. Then it went black.

"Did you see her? *La bella signorina?*" Fuglio said, pulling out Alex's sunglasses and putting them on.

"Hey, that's *my* girl, *bambino*. Tell me what you know about the Putifaros."

Chapter Four

Mission Accomplished

"Brent, there's no room in this van. Where are we going to sit?" said Jennalee.

Brent heard the frustration in Jennalee's voice and peered through the open door of the rusted van. Rachel peeked inside, too. Their heads nearly touched.

With her so close, the memory of when he first met the petite girl with the brunette French braids flooded back. She'd driven a similar van and got it cornered in a dangerous slum of Buenos Aires. He and his missionary companion, Ammon, had helped her and her friends escape.

"We'll have to squish," Rachel said, stepping back, her face flushed. "You and Jennalee can have the back. Just shift the boxes onto your laps. I'll fit in front."

"At least you're not *driving* this time," he said, with a sideways smirk.

Rachel laughed. "Did I ever thank you for getting me out of that situation?"

"Yes, but I wouldn't mind hearing it again."

"You rescued us, Brent, you really did."

She looked so pretty, but beyond physical beauty, she was kind and honorable in everything she did. Brent tried to get his mind back to the rescue at hand.

Jennalee offered to ride in front.

"I'm warning you," said Rachel, "it's uncomfortable up there in the middle even with a pillow."

"No worries. It's a better spot for me to look for Alex. I can see the whole road from there."

"Climb on in, sweetheart," said Judy, opening her door. "Sorry, no seatbelts."

Brent snickered. "You remember we rode a pile of scooter parts up the mountain. No seatbelts on it either. I'd better go park it."

"The hotel staff mentioned they'd keep your motorbike locked in the back of the restaurant without a charge since we're going to help in Taurasi," Judy said.

"Great." Brent walked the scooter to the back of the building where a hotel worker, shrugging that he knew no English, shook his hand. It took more than a few minutes of awkward communication to lock the motorbike in a shed. He found out the Italian language wasn't even slightly like the Castilian Spanish of Argentina.

Brent climbed into the back seat with Rachel, who broke his grin when she plopped a large box on to his lap. They settled themselves around crates of water, food, and medical supplies.

The van sped up the road and Rachel looked at him from behind her box. "Wish we had some *Dulce de Leche* ice cream about now."

"Me, too. There's one thing I regret about Argentina. I never learned to dance the most famous dance ever, the tango." *Except with a broom.*

Rachel looked at him harder. "So, you dance? I mean . . ."

"Why are you so surprised?"

"I thought Mormons were forbidden to dance. I mean, they don't allow other things, like coffee or tea or alcohol."

He snickered. "There's a lot you don't know about us. BYU's Musical Dance Theatre program is one of the best."

Jennalee got into the conversation from the front. "Dancing's part of our heritage. Joseph Smith was a great dancer, and our grandfather Brigham Young, loved to dance, too. The story goes he'd have the furniture removed from the sitting room at Beehive House so his family could dance together."

Rachel looked pensive. "Hmm . . . I never connected your last name with Brigham Young."

"It's no big deal," Jennalee said, "we're the 4th greats and there are hundreds of us."

Rachel didn't answer, and Brent felt a need to explain.

"If you're thinking there are so many Youngs because of polygamy, you're right. It's historical fact. We don't deny it."

"I didn't want to be rude," said Rachel. "Of course, there must be lots of kids. Depending on how many wives, I suppose."

Jennalee chimed into the conversation again. "Brigham Young had 46 children who lived into adulthood. I guess in Utah, we grow up with the idea, but polygamy's no longer practiced, at least in the official LDS Church."

"I see," said Rachel. "But it's still in existence, isn't it?"

"Yes," said Brent. "I'm sure you've heard of the Fundamentalist LDS sect on the border of Utah and Arizona."

"Yes, I even read a book about them. Don't they follow the original religion?"

Old feelings of shame overwhelmed Brent and he felt his ears get hot. "Yes, they're going by what Joseph Smith taught. I'll just say it. It's wrong. It's been a blight on the Church since the beginning. Polygamy's one of the reasons I started examining church history at the BYU library."

Rachel nodded slowly. "Want some gum?" she asked, digging in a tiny purse. "Oh, look what else I found." She held up an old iPod and cord. She passed it up to Jennalee, who plugged it into the lighter, and praise songs soon filled the uncomfortable silence.

Brent took a piece of gum, and chewed on it . . . and on the subject of polygamy. He was only nine or ten when he found out what it was, but Brent *knew* it couldn't be sanctioned by God the way the Prophets had said. Maybe that was when most of his doubts started.

It was embarrassing to talk to Rachel about the bad things about Mormonism, but his shame went out the window as he listened to the music. He suddenly felt connected to this warm group of evangelical Christians. Brent reflected on how the lyrics were directed *to* the Lord in contrast to the hymns he was familiar with. Those seemed to be *about* God or the Prophet, Joseph Smith.

His sister must've thought so, too. Between songs, she said, "You don't know how great it is for us to hear these songs."

Rachel said, "You have the Mormon Tabernacle Choir. They sing like this, don't they?"

His sister shrugged. "Yes, but . . . most songs and hymns they sing aren't at all like these. There's a modern feeling with yours. And this music takes you deeper."

"You have Christian radio in Utah, right?" Rachel asked.

Brent said, "Yes, I used to listen to it in my car sometimes. And I heard a few modern Christian songs in the dentist's office, chosen to agree with *our* religion if you get my drift. It seems mainline Christian music has yet to be fully approved by Church leaders. We categorize ourselves as a Christian group outside Protestantism and Catholicism. We've been warned the secular world could take away our faith."

"Secular?"

"Which means anything outside Mormonism. But we've chosen not to fear it any more, haven't we, Jenn?"

The praise music stopped when Judy said, "Next exit, Jerry. Taurasi, here we come."

With the late afternoon sun streaming out from behind clouds, a quiet peace settled in the van in anticipation of the work ahead.

Shifting the box on his lap, Brent loosened the flaps to peek inside: medical supplies, antibiotics, bandages, and butterfly stitches. He memorized the contents. The more he knew where to find stuff, the better he'd be able to help fast, even if he hadn't attained Eagle Scout like Ammon.

When he'd met Rachel during his mission, he was bewildered for a time about what it meant to *know* Jesus. His LDS rote-learning about the Savior capsized. He felt he was at the bottom of despair one night a few months before the end of his mission. While Ammon slept, Brent prayed hard against the black night suffocating him with depression and confusion. He cried out to Jesus to save him out of the darkness. And then, sobbing on his knees on the cold floor, begging for Jesus to forgive his sins and be his only Master, Brent knew he was changed. Forever.

Next to him was the knockout of a woman who'd dared to tell him things about God he'd resisted at first. Rachel was righteously fierce about spreading the biblical Good News, but she also had a gentle convincing way. Back then, she told him that 'Truth will stand up to any investigation.'

Thump! Thump! The sound of the tires thudding on a metal bridge snapped his head up to see what lay ahead. There were rocks on the road, thrown there by the quake. Jerry drove on, dodging obstacles as they approached the shattered town of Taurasi. A police roadblock halted them and Jerry stopped the van and rolled down the window.

Jennalee explained that they had medical supplies and were aid workers from America. The officials shook their heads, looking doubtful. One of the police officers opened the back door and looked through a few boxes. A loud discussion with the other officers ensued. He finally waved them forward in a sweeping motion.

"Better hurry before they change their minds," Jennalee whispered.

The van inched forward on the torn-up tarmac until the road's fissures became too wide for them to pass, so Jerry steered onto a narrow dirt-packed road leading uphill through a vineyard and parked. The setting sun now threw rosy hues, making long shadows, but they got out and began to unload, knowing darkness would soon overtake their efforts.

Strings of refugees had settled in the vineyard for the night, eyes staring ahead, their faces streaked with dirt. An old man with a cane limped by. He saw Brent and Rachel and asked, *"Americano?"*

"Si," Brent answered, hoping he could at least understand him, if not speak to him. Jennalee stepped up to interpret.

The man pointed with his cane to a ruined stone fortress on a rocky cliff and murmured something. Then he headed downhill, shaking his head.

"He said the castle fell. It's been there since the tenth century," said Jennalee.

"The tenth century?" said Rachel, "We need to brace ourselves for what we find. Only a massive quake could knock an ancient castle down."

"Please tell us what Alex looks like," Jerry said, "so we can find him."

Jennalee's face clouded a little. "Last I saw, blood covered his curly brown hair. Alex is not quite as tall as Brent. His clothes are tattered rags. There's a little boy with him and a hurt young man."

"Okay. Bring water for as many as you can. They've been out here a long time without it," said Jerry. "Judy and I will set up tents."

Brent took a crate of water bottles, and Jennalee and Rachel grabbed boxes of medical supplies, and headed up the dirt road to the town. Halfway up to the town wall, they caught sight of a couple of bedraggled-looking men under a large-leafed tree. One man lay curled up on the ground and one stood, with his hand blocking the setting sun. A small boy loitered around him.

Jennalee halted mid-stride, bumping Brent's arm. "It's him! It's the skinny little boy . . . the one with Alex!"

Brent put the water down at his sister's shriek. The standing man with wild hair came out of the deep shade, squinting. He walked towards them. Jennalee dropped her box and broke into a wild run.

Chapter Five

So Close to Heaven

"Alex!" Jennalee shouted, running as fast as she could.

It was miraculous. The Almighty God had answered her. No one could have intervened except her big God, when he led them to the exact place where Alex waited for help. Down to her toes, she felt his great love for her.

When she reached Alex, he swept her into his arms, holding her a long time, close and tight, as if he'd never let her go. He caressed her hair and kissed the top of her head again and again. She didn't care that he smelled of caked blood and dirt and sweat.

Unsteady on his legs, Alex separated from her, and held her by the shoulders. He flashed his familiar crooked smile. "What are you doing here? You're supposed to be on your mission! How'd you find me, Jenn?"

"When I knew you'd been kidnapped, I had to run away from my mission. And today I saw you on camera, on the BBC, and the building behind you collapsed. . . I thought you'd been killed."

They both started to talk at once and she let him speak first.

"Fuglio screamed '*Andiamo*', and got me out of my freeze. But the reporter and his cameraman were underneath the . . . oh, Jenn, I feel dizzy." He sunk to his knees.

The boy grasped Alex's arm and Jennalee crouched down beside him. "Alex? Can you hear me?"

His dazed face appeared as though he couldn't. "Massimo. Help him first.

Needs antibiotics. And this boy needs. . .”

“Don't worry, Alex, we'll take care of them. Now lie down here, and we'll carry you out.”

The boy, who had to be Fuglio, pierced the air with a wail as she helped Alex lie down in the dirt, where he lost consciousness. But he still breathed, Jennalee made sure of it.

She reverted to the boy. “Don't cry. He's not dead, only unconscious.”

Fuglio still sobbed, unable to control it.

Alex must've run out of strength after waiting all day for help. Jennalee poured water on gauze and dabbed at his pale face, trying to get rid of the blood, the injury, the trauma.

Brent caught up to her, saying, “I'll get the stretchers. Judy's working on the short guy, but she'll be over here soon. She's a nurse, you know.”

Within a minute, Judy knelt next to Alex, feeling his head. “Nasty head wound. Hand me some scissors and a razor. I can't tell if his skull is fractured because of his hair.”

Rachel had come running with a box and she handed Judy the needed tools.

Judy went to work on Alex's full head of hair, now a tangled mix of wet and dried blood. He didn't look like a prosperous businessman anymore; his elegant suit unrecognizable, the rich fabric torn at the knees. He'd lost weight and a filthy silk shirt accentuated his ribs.

Jennalee asked, “What about the other man, Massimo?” She pointed to Alex's feverish companion.

Judy answered, “I've given him a shot of antibiotics for his pneumonia, one of the worst cases I've seen as a nurse. He needs a hospital, though. As for this guy, don't wash his head; the wound is trying to congeal. You can wash the blood from his face and chop off what hair you can around the wound. I found no obvious fractures, but the doctors will find them if they're there. Let's roll him onto the gurney and you, Mr. Young, can drive him to the hospital in Naples. *Carefully*.”

She handed the van's keys to Brent. “You'll also drive a young mother with a broken arm and her baby. Jerry and I will stay here until you come back tomorrow. I'm sure we'll have more patients for you. See the credit card attached to the keys? You'll need to fill up whenever you can. And bring more water and supplies when you come."

They laid Alex on the metal floor of the back of the empty YWAM van, and next to him, Massimo. Jennalee climbed in and cushioned their heads with wadded up blankets. She set cool wet cloths on each of their foreheads. Fuglio bounded in beside her, his eyes never leaving his hero.

A young woman, her mouth pinched in pain and her arm in a sling, got into the middle seat with her toddler, who promptly fell asleep. Rachel sat in front next to Brent, who adjusted his mirrors. At the last moment, Judy seated another woman with an injured shoulder next to the child.

"Judy, doesn't Alex have a concussion? Shouldn't we keep him awake?" Jennalee asked before the door shut.

"Not necessary," Judy said. "Wake him when you get to the Naples hospital; drive fast now and Godspeed."

Brent sped downhill into what had become a black night. Her brother would have to do some maneuvering to get through the emergency vehicles and earthquake damaged roads. No one would get any sleep that night, except maybe the injured.

In an hour, the thin light from a rising full moon illuminated the passengers inside the van's dark interior. Jennalee could make out Fuglio's liquid eyes. Thinking he was about to cry, she stroked his shock of hair. The boy cringed and ducked under her touch, crouching close to his cinch bag.

Then, in Italian, Fuglio pointed at her and said, "You are the *Signorina* on the mobile phone."

"What phone?"

Rummaging in the sack next to his toothpick-like legs, the boy pulled out a red-covered cell phone with a black screen.

"I found it. It's mine!" Fuglio shouted.

"It's alright. Calm yourself. It's Alessandro's," she answered with a gentle tone as Rachel whirled around to see what was going on. "Give it to me," she said.

Fuglio let her pry it from his fingers.

"Rachel, will you charge this a little?"

Jennalee passed the phone up, stretching her arm above the two women and child, now asleep in spite of the jostling ride.

In the front, Rachel set the phone on the dash where the sulking Fuglio could see it. A dim light shone from the screen.

"Where did you find it, Fuglio?" asked Jennalee, vaguely remembering something about Alex retrieving it on the day he disappeared. "Alex told me he lost it. You can trust me."

The boy wouldn't look at her, but his eyes glittered with a hint of fun. "I find at a woman's house."

"What woman?"

"Alessandro get dressed in a suit to go there in his fancy car." Passing car lights showed his grin with two absent front teeth.

"Why did he leave his phone there?"

"I don't know, but she have it, the woman."

"What is her name?"

Fuglio shrugged like only an Italian can. "She not nice woman, she hit me. Her name was Caprice Putifaro. My uncle hits me, too." He pointed to his eye and in the moonlight, she could see the dark blue shadow of a recent bruise.

"I'm so sorry, Fuglio. That's awful, horrible . . . what's the word in Italian?"

"*Brutto.*" He winced as though remembering the hit.

"*Si*, ugly is a good word for brutish people who hit kids. What does Alex have to do with this woman?"

His little eyebrows shot up. "Business. *Vino.*"

"When did you take the phone?"

Fuglio hesitated. "I no remember. After Alessandro was gone. See what he give to me?" Out of his bag, he pulled out Alex's expensive designer sunglasses. "He want to go inside Massimo's jail. Alex want to help him. Very sick, is Massimo."

She glanced at Massimo's sweaty face in the moonlit van. She could hear shallow breathing as he slept alongside Alex, both lying on the cold floor in the back of the van.

Fuglio took a deep breath. "The *Camorra* not want Massimo to die because they get money from his father. His father is *Signore* Bonadelli! You know, the rich one in the magazines?" The flow of his Italian with its musical cadences poured out.

"I see. How long were they locked up?"

"Alessandro? Not so long. Massimo, long time. He will probably die."

"Don't say that. They'll save Massimo at the hospital, and Alex, too. My brother is driving them there, very fast."

It nagged at her, the thought of this woman having Alex's phone. Who was she? What if Alex had *been* with other women? What if she'd left her mission only to find out he hadn't been true to her?

She was sure Alex could explain, but an unrelenting suspicion crept into her mind. For starters, there was the tall, richly dressed woman at the bank, Firenza, who seemed to know Alex quite well.

She remembered the fight they'd had the night before he was kidnapped. Now, with what Fuglio said, it looked like Alex might have wandered from her, no matter what he'd told her.

Jennalee glanced at her ring shining by the light of the city outskirts. Could she still tell him 'Yes' even if he'd strayed from her?

She saw Alex move his hand in his sleep, searching for Massimo. Surely he was too kind, too good, to go out on her, wasn't he?

She thought of the Bible verse she'd tried to memorize on the back of the scooter. It was Philippians 4:8. ". . . *Whatever is true, whatever is noble, whatever is honorable, whatever is right, whatever is pure, whatever is admirable—if anything is excellent or praiseworthy—think about such things*". And for her, Alex was all those things.

Fuglio yawned, his two missing teeth showing. She decided to tackle a different line of questioning.

"Fuglio, who kidnapped Alex? Your uncle?"

The boy motioned for her to lower her ear to his mouth, and whispered, "*Si*, orders. He do what the *Camorra* bosses say." He put his finger to his lips. "Tell no one." Then he swiped across the base of his neck with a finger.

It unnerved her, sitting there in the back of the van, to think of the danger

Alex had endured. And this little boy, too.

"It's charged one bar," said Rachel. "By the way, awesome picture, Jennalee." Rachel put the cell phone on the rear seat where it lit up with Jennalee's senior picture as the background.

Fuglio's look of amusement became a frown when Jennalee grabbed the phone and held it tightly in her own hand. "Fuglio, this is important. Did you say Massimo's last name was Bonadelli?"

"*Si*, the famous businessman."

Using Alex's phone, she texted Lucio the information so he could locate Massimo's family. Next, she searched old texts for the one sent to the missionary phone she shared with her companion on the night of Alex's disappearance. She'd been in her bed that fateful night when the threatening text came through. It read: *You'll never find him.*

Now she stared at the words that had caused her to flee in order to find Alex, knowing he was in grave danger. She suspected Caprice Putifaro was the sender.

Fuglio still glared at her.

"What about you, Fuglio? Your parents must be looking for you. I can call them."

"Me? I go where Alessandro goes. He takes care of me. Ah . . . here is Napoli."

Her first sight of the city of Naples was like a dream, lit up end to end, with a sparkling harbor. It was easy to conclude that Neapolitans loved night life. The city streets were as busy as any other city would be during the daytime.

At every sign announcing 'Ospedale,' Brent pressed the gas to the floor, and Jennalee steadied herself in the back. When he finally stopped the van at the emergency entrance, Alex sat up, mumbling. The back door was opened by hospital staff and Alex got out with support from Brent. A nurse made him sit in a wheelchair. Hospital workers scrambled to care for Massimo, the women passengers, and the child.

"I did some crazy fast driving to get here," Brent said to Alex, "by the way, I'm Brent Young."

Alex extended his hand and Brent shook it.

His words slurring, he said, "You have no idea how glad I am to see you. N . . . no idea." He put his hand on his head. "Jenn, text my Mom, and t . . . tell her I'm okay." Then he slumped in the wheelchair, and a nurse seized the chair handles and ran through the emergency double doors.

■   ■   ■

Rachel hugged Jennalee in the waiting room. "Let's pray."

Feeling drained, Jennalee managed to stay strong while they held hands and implored God to bring healing and help the work in Taurasi. Fuglio listened with head bowed. As they sat down in plastic chairs, Rachel's phone buzzed, and she went outside to take the call. Brent stared at his smart phone, sliding on the screen with his fingers.

"What are you looking at?" asked Jennalee, her curiosity piqued.

"The news. Massimo's been on the front pages for a month. The youngest son of Sergio Bonadelli, a prominent Roman businessman, was kidnapped in broad daylight after soccer practice in Rome. The family thought he was dead because they never heard about any ransom from the kidnappers."

"Oh my heck, this happened in Rome? Where *aren't* the mafia in Italy?"

"Jenn, did you remember to call Uncle Lucio?"

"I did," she answered, "and he'll be here in a couple hours."

Without Alex, Fuglio followed Brent like a lost puppy, finally landing on his lap, where he fell asleep.

"I sure miss home, and our brothers," she said, watching the boy curl up next to Brent's chest.

"Yeah. Do you think anything will ever be the same at home, Jenn? If things go badly, I don't think Mom and Dad will want us to see much of those little guys."

It was a real possibility. Their parents might consider them to be bad influences since they'd left the faith. Her exhausted mind pushed away the thought.

Rachel came back inside and sat next to Brent. She slipped off Fuglio's torn-up sneakers as he slept. They waited in silence until Lucio, looking rather disheveled, entered the waiting room with a stout man in a fitted gray suit.

Lucio argued at the desk, in heated Italian, finally turning back to the waiting room in defeat. The other man was allowed inside.

With a friendly nod at Brent, Uncle Lucio kissed the girls' hands in a grand gesture. "They will not let me see my nephew," he said.

Brent said, "They're busy doing tests to make sure Alex has no bleeding on his brain or fractures. They won't let us in, either."

Lucio waited without a shred of patience, tapping his foot, until an unlucky nurse came out of the double doors. "Take me to my nephew!" he said, waving Euros at her.

"Family?" she asked, looking with disdain at the money.

Lucio shouted, "*Zio!* Uncle!"

Waving away the cash, she led him back through the swinging doors. He motioned for them to follow, but the nurse wagged a finger at them. "One at a time," she said.

Jennalee slumped back into her plastic chair. Half an hour later, Lucio strode out of the double doors like a cowboy in a bar.

"Alessandro will be fine. He has a concussion, I think you call it. They stitched up his head. His brain is not bleeding and there are no fractures. He needs a night of rest; no one else can see him tonight." He made a grandiose gesture with his arms. "So, my tired Americans, I have hotel rooms for us at my friend Alfonso's high-rise. Follow me. *Momento*, who is this dirty little boy?"

Chapter Six

Before the Snow Flies

When Alex woke up he was propped up with pillows in a hospital bed, and a food tray was in front of him. He blinked. A place behind his eyes pounded dully, and he tried to remember what had happened.

Shifting position, he spied Jennalee, reading a book in a chair next to his bed, her face soft and pink-cheeked. This had to be a dream. He squeezed his eyes closed then re-opened them. She was still there.

A boy's voice chirped, "No more sleeping for Alessandro!"

Fuglio stood on the other side of his bed, his impish face smiling.

Flashbacks trickled into Alex's tired brain. Earthquakes and equally terrorizing aftershocks. The collapse of the Red Cross building. Waiting for help under the fig tree. Jennalee running to him.

A groan escaped him. "What day is it?"

Jennalee's face faded in and out until she was close enough to squeeze his hand. "Alex, you've been in the hospital for two days. You had a severe concussion and needed stitches."

He felt his wounded head. The open gash had become a bald spot with a jagged line of catgut threads.

"I must look like Frankenstein," he said.

Jennalee beamed. "It doesn't matter, you're still my Alex."

Fuglio jumped up on the bed and perched like a little bird beside him, looking happy and somber at the same time.

"Told you I wouldn't die," Alex said.

The boy sniffed. Being quiet was out of character for him.

"Everything's a blur, Jenn. Where's Massimo?"

"He's here, too. He had pneumonia and is still weak, but much better."

Alex let out a groan. "We had no help until you came. I couldn't believe my eyes it was you, Jenn. How did you make it to Taurasi?"

"You don't remember? I told you. I saw you on the BBC with my brother. We came with his friend Rachel, who's in YWAM. They had a van, and . . ."

"I remember the van. I didn't want to get into another van."

"No wonder. When you were kidnapped, witnesses said the mafia forced you into a van."

"My head hurts. Did they find a skull fracture?"

"No fracture, just a serious concussion."

"If this is what it's like to have a concussion, I don't ever want another one." He pushed the food away. "You eat it, Jenn."

"I already had lunch. Eat a bite or two, Alex, or Fuglio will inhale it, even though he already had lunch." The street urchin handed a slice of cheese to him with a tepid smile.

Alex put it in his mouth, but there was no taste, just saltiness. "Where's Uncle Lucio? Did he call Mom?"

Jennalee nodded. "Lucio's around here someplace. And I just let your mom know you woke up. It's the middle of the night in Utah so she'll call you later. All flights from Salt Lake have been cancelled because of a storm and she can't come right away."

"Tell her I'm okay, she doesn't need to come."

"She'll wait for the weather to clear," said Jennalee, "then she'll be here. And your Uncle Lucio came through with first-class accommodations for us the last two nights, complete with an American breakfast."

She paused. "Alex, Fuglio found your cell phone. It's charged now." She dug it out of her purse.

"My lost cell phone? Oh yeah. He had it." Alex paused, looking at the boy chowing down on his plate. "Did you look at it, Jenn?"

"Mm-mm."

Awkwardness hung in the air so long, it was interrupted by an orderly taking the food tray away just as Fuglio finished chomping a sandwich.

"We'll talk about it later, Alex . . . when your head doesn't hurt."

His aching brain scrambled to find out what she'd seen. "I can explain it all. It's complicated, Jenn, but heck, our lives have been crazy since the day we met."

"You need to rest," she said, standing.

Loud knocking cut off his next thought. Uncle Lucio swept into the room, grabbed his face and kissed him on both cheeks. A dozen people poured into the room, some placing flowers at his feet. Nonna came in with the boy cousins. Camera phones clicked. He lost track of Jennalee in the melee.

Boldly stepping up to his bed, a balding man in a three-piece suit boomed, "I am Sergio Bonadelli." He had a unique accent, sort of British-Italian. "I am Massimo's father. Thank you, thank you for saving my son. He is alive because of you."

The man yanked his hand up and down in a firm handshake and Alex didn't know what to say.

Sergio's hands moved as he spoke. "Massimo said you let go of a chance to escape. Instead, you chose to help him. You carried him all the way to Taurasi."

"Well, a scooter helped a lot . . . I'm no hero, sir," Alex said, seeing Massimo smile weakly from his wheelchair as he was pushed into the crowded room.

"Oh, but you are. The doctors say Massimo had only hours to live when he was brought in."

"*Signore*," said Alex, "Jennalee and her brother Brent are the ones who . . ."

"Yes, yes. They helped, too. And this little boy, even he helped. We are looking after him while we search for his relatives."

Alex remembered he'd promised to look for them, too. He glanced at his little follower, who grinned, crumbs clinging to the tip of his long nose. What a relief that the Bonadellis had taken him in.

Signore Bonadelli continued, "I talk with your girlfriend here last night."

The Italian gentleman looked at Jennalee and cleared his throat. "If I were you, I would marry her tomorrow!" He winked. Lucio guffawed and clapped his hands and everyone followed with a loud applause. Pink splotches appeared on Jennalee's neck.

Alex felt his head, his fingers finding his stitches. "We'll have to wait. She doesn't want to be the bride of Frankenstein."

■ ■ ■

A week later, in his bedroom at the family villa near Rome, with Nonna fussing over him and Lucio constantly apologizing, Alex felt stronger. Doctors had ordered plenty of rest, and Jennalee enforced it.

Somehow, he'd broken the news to Lucio he was going back to America. Too much had happened here, some good, and some very bad. He wanted his American life back, with his old truck and friends in Utah.

Alex longed to start college to fulfill his dream of a medical career, even though he knew he could never afford the tuition. He had the grades and grit but no money. And student loans would set him back for years. He sighed, knowing loans would be the only recourse since he no longer earned the salary of a European wine merchant.

Tracing his hand across the carved wooden framing around the diamond-shaped window panes, he reflected on the three hundred-year-old Giovanini villa which had been part of his life since he'd been born. He used to miss it terribly when his family was moving around America and he was forced to change schools.

But he had to admit America was his true home. Looking between the panes, he saw Jennalee walk up the long cypress-lined drive like a fairy-tale princess, and he wanted to swoop her up on a white stallion and take her to his castle . . . or married student housing. Would she still have him?

He climbed into bed and leaned against the pillows as she came through the open door, her cheeks flushed with color. She wore a blue sweater matching her eyes.

Now he knew how the Beast had felt around Beauty. His hand flew up to hide his ugly wound. He felt short bristles of hair at odd angles around the lumpy scar that itched something fierce. How long would he have this swath of hair mown from his head?

"Don't worry, your hair will grow," she said like she'd read his mind. "I think it makes you look kind of . . . well . . ."

"C'mon, Jenn, I look like a freak."

"Alex, am I such a shallow person that I'd care about some missing hair and stitches?" she scolded. "All that matters to me is you're alive. And this proves it."

She held up her left hand with his grandmother's ruby and diamond ring.

"As you can see, my answer to your proposal is 'Yes.' I waited until now to tell you, since you were still recovering and kind of in shock."

He took her hand, staring at the ring. "Does this mean you want to marry me? Are you sure?"

Her entire head moved in an emphatic nod. "Yes!" she answered. "Alex, I want to be your wife, but here you go, acting strange."

"Jenn, I thought I had everything figured out. Now I don't know."

She took her hand away, and twisted the ring with her fingers. "What do you mean? Because . . . when you were unconscious, I was right there by your bedside when you said some awfully weird things."

"Uh-oh. I did?"

"You released me from any promises I made and told me you weren't good enough for me. I think it was the head injury talking. Was it?" Her brow furrowed.

"It wasn't the head injury, Jenn, I meant every word." His heart pumped faster, remembering what a jerk he'd been while he worked for his uncle. He had unfinished business with Jennalee and had to tell her the truth. He felt miserable inside. "Let's go for a walk in the vineyard and I'll explain my thoughts."

He put on a long robe and slipped on his shoes. Neither spoke as they stepped out of the French doors at the back of the house and holding hands, slowly roamed to the vineyard's dirt road. His legs shook, and feeling dizzy, he leaned against Jennalee's arm and focused his eyes on the winter vines shorn of grapes, and their cold, dead leaves. Clouds dimmed the sunlight, an appropriate backdrop for his dull spirits.

"We don't need to go far, Alex. What do you have to tell me?"

"I'm just so sorry, Jennalee," he blurted out. "I was a selfish jerk when I pushed you to leave your mission. You must have felt pressured to give it up because I didn't want to wait eighteen months. And I don't want you . . . agreeing to marry me if it's because I coerced you."

"You have nothing to be sorry for. I never felt forced by you." She sounded like she meant it.

"Hear me out. Back in Provo, when I realized you'd taken on a mission, I felt totally rejected. In my mind, the Church had you, and I'd lost you forever. I was angry, Jenn. You hurt my ego and I couldn't see a future for us. So I gave up and started living a different way here in Italy."

She put her hand out to stop him. "Alex, it's me who should be sorry. When you flew back to Utah to find me, I should've left everything to go with you. If I had, maybe none of this would've happened."

"Jenn, it was me. I pushed you to give up your whole life. And it's not fair. I acted like a controlling bully." He paused. "I still hope you'll have me, but you need to decide free of me, on your own volition."

Her face was hidden by her blowing hair. Worse yet, she said nothing, until her quiet voice drifted to his ears. "I'm wearing your ring, Alex, and the cross you gave me. I *have* decided and my answer is still 'Yes'."

"You need to think this out, Jenn. You're not obligated to me."

Abruptly, Jennalee stopped walking and crossed her arms, there on the vineyard path. "Okay, you've given me your perspective. Now listen to mine. I didn't go into the Missionary Training Center with the best of intentions. I went because I had to escape my parents and Bridger Townsend, who was sure I was going to marry *him*. Brent's suggested a mission. He's sorry now, of course."

"*Brent* told you to dodge your parents' wishes by doing a mission?" Her brother had to be one of the nicest, most devious and clever guys ever.

"He couldn't see a way out for me. I couldn't either," she said, taking his arm again. "Don't you see? God used you back in Utah to show me a new way to live, and now I want to live it. God brought us together again, Alex, and I believe we're meant for each other."

"Jenn, remember the last night we were together before my kidnapping? On the Via Margutta in front of your apartment? You told me I was arrogant and all I cared about was money. And you were right."

She frowned. "Alex, you weren't like that until you came to Rome and started wearing European suits and shiny ostrich shoes and meeting rich people like the woman at the bank."

"My shoes aren't ostrich."

"Well, that woman is tall enough to be one."

Alex had to laugh. "Firenza *is* tall, especially in heels."

They'd climbed the slope, and were now far into the vineyard. "Let's go back," he said, aiming his direction to view the ancient vine-covered villa at the bottom of the hill.

"Jenn, see our house? Money is what my uncle needs to keep this place going. I started out trying to please him, going through the motions, but it wasn't long before I got sucked into a life I not only liked, but *loved*."

"So I was right? You really did change from the kind and generous guy I knew in Utah into a snobbish European businessman?"

"Yes. You've got to understand I was mourning you. I thought I'd lost you forever. And I tried to replace you with the high life. But I took the wrong road, away from what God had for me. I'm sorry for taking that path, Jenn."

She was silent for a full minute, studying his eyes. "Did your wrong road include other women? Because I saw your phone calls and texts."

"There was no other woman . . . those calls were business only. If you're talking about Firenza, she's not my type. I can truthfully say, nothing happened with *any* woman."

"Alex, I'm not the only woman who thinks you look like a male model on a magazine cover whether you're wearing an Italian suit or T-shirt and jeans. You'd better tell me about the older lady, *Signora* Caprice Putifaro. Her number's all over your phone history."

"That rascal Fuglio told you about her, didn't he? For a kid, he knows an awful lot. I don't know what he said, but nothing happened. On my side anyway. She *did* try to kiss me, against my will. And I had to get out so fast I accidentally left my phone."

He saw Jennalee's smug look, under her wind-blown hair.

"Does this mean I have no rivals? Are you really all *mine*, Alex?"

Even though she was saying these wonderful words, complete trust eluded him.

"Jennalee, there's no one else in my life but you. The question is . . . will *you* be all *mine* when we get back to Utah?"

"What do you mean? Of course, I will. We're engaged now."

He gulped. Her parents would be upset by their engagement and she could waver. "I have a burning question for you. This time, are you all in? Even if you miss your old life and your family doesn't understand? Will you stick with me or go back to them?"

She declared, "I decided already when I put on your ring." She took his arm again in a strong almost-hug and some of his skepticism melted.

"Don't get me wrong," she said, "I've waded through plenty of confusion about religion. But I haven't yet told you . . . what happened the same day you disappeared. And how it makes all the difference."

She related to him how her companion's heel had developed a blister and they stopped at a church with a catacomb, and she walked in the garden praying . . . when, a strong warm wind roiled all around her.

"And in that wind," she said, "was unbelievable, unconditional, powerful love that gave me a supernatural hug directly from Jesus. After that I was filled with absolute joy."

That pure joy was still on her face. Why hadn't he noticed it earlier? Jennalee possessed a new joyful faith in Jesus. She wasn't being influenced by mere humans like himself anymore; she was clearly following Jesus on her own.

"Alex, it was a gift, a true born-again experience, not caused by any pressure from you or any human being. The real presence of Jesus came and filled me with his love from the top of my head to my toes. I've never felt anything like it before and I'm surrendered to it."

He took her in his arms and hugged her, close and tight, feeling her warmth. "Oh, Jenn, it was the best day in your life and one of the worst days in mine, but I'd do it again in a minute for this outcome."

"You'll help me learn about this new faith, won't you?"

"It's a new *life*, Jenn. Forget any of man's religion. Knowing Jesus is just the beginning, then we learn how to walk with him and practice our faith. And we'll do it together, in Utah. We'll find a place to worship we both agree on."

A pale sun appeared above the dissipating fog and beams of yellow light poured between the clouds, and hit earth. Neither of them had any words, struck dumb with pure reverence of what God had done in their lives.

When they reached the hedge surrounding the iron gate to the garden, Alex told her how he'd cried out to God, alone in his mafia dungeon. "My Father disciplined me. He had to because I wouldn't have listened to him any other way. I closed my heart because of my love for money. It really *is* the root of all kinds of evil, Jenn."

She opened the gate for him. "We're free now, Alex. For me, Jesus is no faraway kind of figurehead anymore. He's a living, close Savior." She lowered her voice. "My past doesn't compare to what I have with Jesus right here, right now."

Hope rose in his soul. "Jenn, I love you, and there's no person on earth I will ever love more than you."

She stretched her neck to kiss his yet unshaved cheek. "I love you, too. And I will be here, like 'our' song says."

He cuddled her close on his chest as they danced slowly among the cypress trees and dormant grapevines, humming the melody of 'their' song, "I Will Be Here". Alex relished the position of her head so close to his heart.

The wind kicked up and a cold white flake landed on her blonde hair. Then another.

"Now that we're together, we can face anything. We've got to get back to Utah," he said, "before the snow flies."

"Hate to tell you, Utah got a foot yesterday."

Chapter Seven
New Plans

Jennalee forgot her worries about going back to Utah when she and Alex entered the warmth of Nonna's Italian country kitchen. Braided garlic hung on a cupboard and a checked tablecloth laden with painted pottery made her feel cozy. Nonna's lasagna and bread, straight from the oven, filled her with gratefulness.

"*Alessandro,* your appetite is back," said Nonna, watching them eat. "And look at you! No more *malato d'amore.*"

"Malady of Love?" asked Jennalee, glancing at him sideways.

He grinned. "I was lovesick from the time I left Utah until now. Nonna nailed it."

At that instant, Brent slid into the kitchen in his stocking feet. As his sister, it was a relief to see him kick off his muddy shoes at the door like he did at home after working outside.

"I can smell lasagna a kilometer away," he said, "you know, point six-zero of a mile."

"You've got a head for numbers," Alex said.

"Not really. I asked Siri. I'm trying to learn metric since I'm working with Lucio spacing the new grapevines."

Nonna handed Brent a heaping plate and patted him on the arm.

Jennalee noticed her brother avoided eye contact with her. "Brent, what's up?" she asked.

He hesitated. "Since you don't have a cell phone, Mom sent you a text on mine late last night. You need to see it." He handed her his phone.

Catching Alex's worried eyes, she took a deep breath and read the text.

"Mom says she bought tickets for Brent and me to fly home . . . oh, no!"

"When?" asked Alex.

"The flight takes off at noon from Rome on December 25. She says they were the cheapest."

Alex looked crushed. "On Christmas? Barely a week away."

She read the next part. "And she told the bishop I left my mission at her request because of family difficulties."

"That's good news, isn't it? You won't be in trouble now," said Alex.

"It *is* a legitimate excuse for leaving, Jenn," said Brent. "It's great of Mom to offer a good reason like that."

"But I don't need excuses. I'm ready to give them the real reason why I left," she said. She glanced at the rest of the message, written mostly in capitals. Handing the phone to Alex, she could still see the blaring statement in her brain: "DAD IS SENDING YOU TO LIVE IN LEHI WITH GRANDMA UNTIL YOU OBEY."

She saw a gray cloud overtake Alex's face as he read it. "I can understand why they're angry, but I wish they'd give us a chance."

Unwanted tears welled up in her eyes. "They're treating me like a child. And I don't need the excuse she gave the bishop."

Brent gave her a pat on the shoulder. "Actually, Mom sort of told them the truth. She does need your help. I told you before, our family's having trouble, Jenn. I don't know what's going on, but something's up."

"Well, even if I do fly home on Christmas, I'm not going to Lehi; I don't care what they say."

Alex took her hand. "Jenn, even if you're banished to Lehi, I'll follow you. We can still be together. Your grandma likes me, remember?"

Brent said, "Yeah, knowing Grandma, she'll help you two, like Nonna does here."

"I know," said Jennalee, "but we're *engaged* and Mom and Dad will have to accept it sooner or later. Alex, you *can* get on our flight, can't you?" She couldn't imagine going without him.

Alex studied his phone for a minute. "Looks like flights are sold out for days. My mom's having the same trouble getting here. But I promise to follow as fast as I can." He smiled his crooked smile. "Maybe we should elope!"

A snicker escaped Jennalee. The idea was silly, but . . .

"I know we can't," said Alex, "but it's a thought." He stood up and opened the freezer. "Any room for dessert, Brent? Looks like Nonna's made a *cassata* ice cream cake."

At those words, Nonna sidled over in her sturdy black shoes, and slammed the freezer door shut.

"*Alessandro, la cassata* is not to eat before *Vigilia di Natale!*"

"Okay, Okay. We'll have it on Christmas Eve," he told her. "*Cassata* is better when aged anyway. All that liqueur."

Nonna clapped her hands and began a long diatribe in Italian.

"You think so?" Alex looked intently at his grandma. "She thinks we should set a wedding date, not elope."

"Now?" Jennalee asked. "Maybe we should."

"We might as well. Nothing happens if you don't plan ahead," said Alex.

A torrent of Italian words came from Nonna. Every once in a while, Alex nodded his head.

"Great idea, Nonna," he said, agreeing with his grandmother by repeating, "*Molto facile.*"

"What's 'very easy'?" asked Jennalee.

"Brace yourself. Nonna says if we went to the Civil Registrar's office in our village we could have a marriage license in four days. We sign everything, go to the consulate, get it translated and wait a day or two for the Consular Officer to certify it. The village mayor could marry us officially on Christmas Eve."

Could getting married be this easy? But her enthusiasm sunk a little. If Alex only knew how long she'd visualized her wedding, every single detail of it. Disappointment rose in her when she thought that her dream wedding would be a small civil ceremony in a suburb of Rome.

Still, it would be a wedding in beautiful Italy on Christmas Eve. And the whole idea felt so free. Maybe she should let go of the ideas she'd had since she was seven. The more she thought about it, the more the old expectations dissipated.

"Marrying now would solve a lot of problems," she said, her chin up.

"And create a few," Brent said, shaking his head. "You know, in Utah."

Jennalee's voice shook more than she wanted it to. "What can they do, Brent, if we're married? We're of legal age, and we'll go to college as married students. Eventually, they'll have to live with it."

Brent softened. "Won't you miss having a big wedding, Jenn?"

She sighed. "That idea's gone. Even if we got married in Utah, everyone would have to accept we wouldn't be married in the temple. We can hold a reception in Utah when we get back." It made her sad to say it. She'd truly said goodbye to her heritage.

"In Italy, a civil ceremony always goes before a religious one, anyway," said Alex. "We can have the religious ceremony in Utah *and* a reception."

"Does the mayor work on Christmas Eve?" she asked.

"He would, because Nonna knows everyone in the village, and he's a lonely bachelor. She'll invite him for dinner. He likes her cooking; he'll be here for sure."

Alex's grandmother winked and laughed when she saw they'd understood her suggestions. Such a co-conspirator; maybe when she was young, she'd experienced this kind of chaotic love.

Jennalee spoke up. "Out of everybody, Nonna, you understand us. Your ruby and diamond ring will be on my finger for as long as I live."

Nonna kissed Alex on both cheeks, and her, too.

"This has to be one of the world's shortest engagements," Brent said with a tight smile.

Chapter Eight

Into the Celestial

The next day dawned clear of rain, and after the preliminary marriage papers were signed at the village offices, Alex suggested they all go sightsee in Rome. He felt sure he could keep up with them.

"Uncle Lucio has a standing offer for us to use his old Fiat any time," he said. "He really wants you two to see more of his Eternal City."

"Do you feel strong enough, Alex?" asked Jennalee.

"Don't worry about me, I'm fine. Only you'd better drive, Brent," he said, climbing into the car.

Brent ran inside to get the keys from Lucio and came out in less than a minute, swinging them in his hand. "Lucio's awesome. He's not only generous with his cars but gave us money for lunch."

In the back, Jennalee spread out maps from her Blue Guide to Rome.

"Would you like to go to Mamertine prison where the Romans locked up the Apostle Paul?" she asked. "A real place from the Bible. I'd like to see it."

"Yes, it's close to the Forum, at the top of Capitoline hill. The Apostle Peter was there, too," said Alex. "I went as a boy and I've never forgotten it."

■　　■　　■

They parked and took a bus to the top of one of the Seven Hills of Rome. As a ten-year-old, walking into this place had excited him as much as exploring a living, breathing Bible. But this time, having been a prisoner himself, Alex

49

keenly felt the reality of incarceration. Two thousand years between him and the Apostle Paul melted away, and he rubbed his sweaty palms together.

Tourist's voices echoed off the dark stone walls and clammy floors as they descended the stairway build in recent times leading to the old cistern dungeon. Paul had no stairway, he'd been lowered down through a manhole with a barred cover. Alex took a deep breath. Was the air this damp and dank in all prisons?

Once down, Alex put his hand on the cold chains on the walls and shuddered.

"Whoa, how did Paul survive in here?" asked Brent. "If they chained him to the wall, how did he write the Epistles?"

"Good question," said Alex, steadying his shaky voice. "He had to have Luke and other friends help him. In Roman times, prisoners weren't given any food. Unless they had friends on the outside, they starved to death."

"How cruel," said Jennalee, "I thought the Romans were more civilized."

"They wanted troublemakers like Paul to be forgotten," said Alex. "But for the last two thousand years, his God-inspired letters have been read continually. Paul was far from forgotten because God's more powerful than human governments."

Brent shook his head. "I just don't know how he was able to be strong in his faith in a dark place like this. I mean, this is suffering for your faith like none other."

Anxiety crept up on Alex as he looked at the rock walls of the prison. He could hardly hold down an urge to run up the stairs and escape into the street outside.

Jennalee took one look at him, and said, "We'd better go back upstairs, Brent, Alex doesn't look so good."

With the help of the iron railing, Alex took the stairs two at a time and reached the cobblestones outside in a flash. Leaning forward, he caught his breath. A light sprinkling of rain began to fall, reviving him a little.

"Are you okay, dude?" asked Brent.

Alex nodded. "I don't know what happened to me in there. I just had to get out."

"Look," Jennalee said, "there's a rainbow." She pointed to a patch of misty sky and Roman umbrella pines.

Alex gazed up at the luminous colors and wonder replaced anxiety. That was it, Paul survived only because he was filled inside with the Spirit of Light, and it carried him through, in spite of the gray walls and stench of prison. He remembered the final letter Paul wrote from this jail.

"Paul knew he was going to die," Alex said, "and he wrote to Timothy, 'I have fought the good fight, I have finished the race, I have kept the faith.'"

Brent and Jennalee looked sad.

"He did it all for the Kingdom of God, not himself," said Alex.

"And didn't he write that nothing can separate us from the love of God?" asked Jennalee.

"And nothing did, not even death. That's what Jesus' cross is all about." Alex was filled with awe. Not only did Paul survive, he held his faith firm under a flashing sword at the moment of his beheading outside Rome's city gates.

■　　■　　■

Caught in a traffic jam on the beltway, Brent pressed on the horn exactly like the Roman drivers.

"Are you sure you're not Italian? You drive just like them," said Alex from the back seat, where Jennalee had insisted he could stretch out and rest.

"Yeah, I drive like this in Utah, too. Hey, it looks like it's going to take a long time to get home," Brent said.

"We could make a side trip, if you're not too tired, Alex," said Jennalee.

"I'm fine. I shouldn't have taken those stairs so fast, but I wanted out of there. Now I'm getting a second wind, so where should we go?"

"We're really close to the new LDS temple, and remember, Alex? A few weeks ago, I told you I'd show it to you."

Alex laughed. "That's right, back when you were a missionary. Let's go, then. Uh . . . my phone says the temple's on Via di Settebagni, the Street of the Seven baths. Wonder if there's any significance in that? Take the next exit, Brent."

■　　■　　■

"Formidable, isn't it?" asked Alex, standing in front of the white pinnacled LDS temple. To him it was like an icicle castle, hard and cold.

"Wow," said Brent. "When the Italian government finally allowed us . . . the LDS Church to build a temple next to the capital city of Christendom, they wanted to make an impact. I'd say they were successful."

"It makes a statement alright," said Alex. "With those sharp points shooting upwards."

He strode forward, down the myriad of steps to the entrance, curious to figure out why temples were so secret.

At his side, Jennalee remained quiet, her face as somber as the overcast sky. Suddenly, she stopped short and pointed ahead.

"Another statement. See it, on the door?"

Framed in the icy stone, a faint cross was painted on the plain brown door.

Brent halted and stared. "I've never seen a cross on a temple before."

"Probably an afterthought," Alex said.

"It's no afterthought," Brent answered. "Temple designs are planned for years. It's an effort to fit into Rome. I, for one, have never seen so many crosses in a city."

Alex couldn't help but notice as they got closer, the *chiaroscuro* cross melted like an optical illusion.

■   ■   ■

"Welcome, visitors. Our last tour begins in five minutes," said a breathless young man in a dark suit. "This is the last day the temple is open to the public. After today, it will be dedicated and closed to those outside our faith."

That would be him, always the outsider, considered unworthy. Alex was familiar with the feeling. Anyway, this enormous palace could be a prison, too; a place where one could be trapped by people-pleasing and man-made rule-obeying.

From a table in the foyer, he picked up a few brochures with portraits of a very handsome Joseph Smith and his lovely first wife, Emma. They looked happy, but Alex knew their history from a book based on historical sources in New York, where they'd met and eloped. The date on the brochure was 1827.

Standing outside ancient Rome near the Appian Way, it seemed to Alex like a date from modern times.

He noticed Brent getting antsy while they waited for the tour to begin. Finally, the former LDS missionary walked up to the young man with a bold step.

"I'm Brent Young," he told the monitor, "I'm a RM, and I'll take my sister and our friend through the temple. We don't have time to wait for the tour."

"May I see your temple recommend?" said the young man.

Brent flushed, and got his wallet out. He showed the man a card, who studied it thoroughly.

"I see you're a Returned Missionary, Elder Young. Of course, you're welcome to go through with your sister and friend," said the guide. "As you know, there are a few roped-off areas the public is not allowed in." He glanced at Alex. "You're required to stay away from those."

Alex dropped the brochures and followed Brent, who led them through palatial rooms filled with plush couches and lit by enormous chandeliers. Even the carpets sparkled white. To Alex, the temple resembled a giant hotel lobby, the fanciest he'd ever seen. He looked into corners for hidden cameras.

They went into a room with ornate upholstered chairs lining the walls, and a small altar in the middle with a kneeler around it. What secret rituals could take place here?

"Is this some kind of throne room?" Alex asked.

Jennalee cleared her throat. "It's a marriage sealing room, where couples are sealed together for time and eternity on their wedding day," she said.

Alex wondered about the impact the room might have on Jennalee, though she seemed nonplussed by it. "You're okay, aren't you, Jenn?"

"Totally. Sure, I always dreamed of a temple wedding, but that was before. Everything's different now." Even so, she seemed in a hurry to move on.

They passed a few doors with fancy ropes on them, saying 'Private' or 'No Admittance'. This palace of secrets began to get on his nerves, and Jennalee and Brent weren't as relaxed as they'd been earlier in the day. Of course, at Mamertine prison, *he'd* been the uptight one.

They entered a room where a large round pool stood in the center of domed opulence. It was held upright on the backs of twelve golden oxen. Not like any Baptistery he'd ever seen, including Italy.

"Why bulls?" Alex asked.

"The oxen symbolize the twelve tribes of Israel. The design is from Solomon's Temple." Brent kept his flat voice low.

"Is this where you baptize the dead, and ask them to join the Church as a last chance?"

Looking down, Brent said, "I'll let you answer that, Jenn."

"We . . . I mean, *they* do baptisms by proxy here," said Jennalee. "We've talked about it before, Alex. The veil between the living and the dead is believed to be thinner here in the temple."

No wonder Alex felt strange, if this was the belief. It greatly troubled him, as it would anyone who knew the Bible.

"Time to go," Jennalee said with false cheer. "You have to see the Celestial Room upstairs."

■　■　■

At the very top of the temple, Jennalee said you were supposed to feel closest to heaven while your feet touched earth. But no matter how Alex tried to get this feeling, the undeniably white expanse of the luxurious Celestial Room didn't give him anything like peace. Instead, his neck hardened with tension.

As a large group of tourists entered the room, Jennalee and Brent pushed past them, back out into the hall. He rushed to catch up.

"What's the matter? Do you want to go now?" Alex said, bumping Jennalee's elbow.

"Too crowded in there. Anyway, we should go, they're closing soon," said Brent, his face in full frown.

They stepped into the swank elevator, and got out on the mezzanine floor where they descended a dazzling staircase back to the chandeliered foyer.

On the bottom stair, Alex suddenly heard a somewhat familiar voice.

Jennalee's missionary companion, Sister McKay, hurried towards them. "Well, well, it's Sister Young!" she repeated.

Alex watched Brent disappear into a crowd and flee out the front door.

"And you, too, isn't it, *Signore* Giovanini? You're together?" She smirked. "I should've known."

"Terrilyn, how are you?" Jennalee said, with sincerity in her voice.

The young woman ignored her greeting. "Why are you still in Rome, Jennalee? I thought you were called home for a family emergency."

The sarcasm in her voice roiled Alex and he came to Jennalee's defense. "*Signorina*, there *was* an emergency. It was because of me." He showed her the scar on his head. "See this? Jennalee came to my aid. And, Sister McKay, I want to apologize for leading you to believe I was investigating your religion. I just wanted to be with my fiancée."

Terrilyn looked shocked. "Fiancée? Wow, you've gone awfully far in a short time. Uh . . . I guess I should offer my congratulations." She displayed a white-toothed grin.

"Thank you," Jennalee said, taking Alex's hand. "I've been wanting to talk to you about what happened. Terrilyn, God has a plan for you and one for me. His plan for me was to stay with Alex, but I was mixed up. I never should have become a missionary."

"Oh, for sure. I agree."

"I hope you forgive my mistake. For my part, I have nothing against you."

Terrilyn's eyebrows shot up. "Sister Young, have you thought about this? You're leaving your faith and family if Alessandro never accepts the Gospel."

"I understand that."

"I met your brother, Elder Young. Now *he* believes; he's a priesthood holder, a returned missionary on the right path. Nothing is going to keep *him* from getting married in the temple." When she mentioned Brent, Terrilyn got a telltale dreamy look in her eyes. "I thought I saw him earlier. Where'd he go?"

Alex and Jennalee shrugged at the same time.

"What's the trouble in your family, Jennalee?" asked Terrilyn. "Anything I can help with?"

"We'll sort it out."

"We are taught God allows trouble for you to learn to regain your sacred covenants."

"Trouble comes to everyone on this broken earth, Terrilyn," said Jennalee, her smile gone.

"But weak faith like yours causes more bad things to happen."

Alex watched pink dots appear on Jennalee's neck and had to intervene. "Sister McKay," he said, stepping up closer, and holding out his hand. "Can I have your hand a moment?"

Terrilyn looked stunned but held out her hand. Alex took it lightly in his, and making a deep bow, he said, "Just so you know, I *am* Italian." He kissed her hand and let it go.

The dumbfounded girl blinked and stared.

"I'm also American, and Jennalee and I met in high school in Utah. In a few days, we're going to be Mr. and Mrs. Alex Campanaro. You see, when I represent my family's business, I use my mother's maiden name, which is Giovanini. For now, *Arrivederci*, enjoy Italy."

Jennalee lifted her eyes to the dazzling chandelier. "Don't worry about me, Terrilyn. I met Jesus in a garden, and he overshadows anything here. *Ciao!*"

They caught up with Brent on the way to the car, and Alex teased, "Admit it, Jenn, you didn't run away for my sake, you had to escape *her*, didn't you?"

Brent howled with laughter. "I've never run so fast in my life."

■　■　■

In the car, a long silence followed and Alex detected the two former Mormons were immersed in deep thought. He hoped Jennalee hadn't taken the things Terrilyn said to heart. But he didn't know what to say, so said nothing out of respect. It surprised him when Brent finally opened up a discussion.

"Remember the secret rooms, Alex?"

"Yes, you couldn't show them to me, so now you'll have to tell me what's in them."

Brent's face went dark at the steering wheel, his eyebrows knit in memory.

"There's not a lot I can tell, but here goes. Before doing a mission, we're required to go to the temple for an endowment ceremony. I'm not supposed to talk about it, but . . . it bothered me." A hint of anger was in his voice.

Alex zeroed in on his soon-to-be brother-in-law's statement. "Why?"

"They say it's *sacred*, not secret, but I found the rituals confusing to say the least."

A sudden honking behind them made Alex jump in his seat.

"Looks like we're stuck bumper to bumper again," he said, "so you have time to tell me anything you want."

"Okay," said Brent. "I know non-Mormons find it hard to understand how everything in LDS life leads to the day you go to the temple. It's hyped up through our childhood. It's the crux of the whole religion. And when I finally got there, it was the biggest let-down ever."

The driver in the car behind them chose the juncture to lay on his horn. Brent inched up a foot or two and continued, "I'm convinced the whole temple experience is based on peer pressure, because I found out I was a spiritual jellyfish compared to everyone else. I had to learn to hide it. Then, I was sent on a mission and inside, I knew I was unworthy. I knew I was full of sin with no way to get rid of it."

"I felt the same way, Brent," said Jennalee.

"Why did you feel so sinful if you were following all the stuff they told you to do?" asked Alex.

"I think it's because their solution to sin fell short. Anyway, at the end of my mission, it came down heavy on me. I felt terribly guilty about thinking my friends and family and my whole faith might be wrong. See, the first thing they told us in the temple was that *all* other churches were untrue. I kept thinking that in two thousand years of Christianity, were there *really* essential truths we had that others didn't? On what basis could *we* claim to be the only ones who were right? I began to question the whole idea of the Restored Gospel."

As Brent gripped the wheel and got up to speed on the beltway, he said, "It didn't help when I went through the temple ordinances and found a completely different religion than the one I grew up in. Somebody at the MTC told me the temple experience would take time to understand, but I still think it's bizarre. I knew that LDS are conditioned to never talk about the bad things, to make the Church look good, but I had to admit the truth, at least to myself."

Jennalee nodded from the passenger seat.

Alex responded slowly. "I don't know what to say, except, in the bible, Jesus confronted religious Pharisees with their know-it-all attitudes. Man's religion is what Jesus came to turn upside down. His message is how to have true relationship with God the Father through himself. But most religious people who thought they were perfect couldn't hear him. Jesus wants nothing less than direct relationship with us, without any middlemen coming between him and us."

"Amen, brother," said Brent, the agitation gone from his face.

Jennalee slipped her hand to the back seat and he took it in his.

Chapter Nine

Ascending Higher

Brent didn't know why he felt so nervous on his way to the train station to pick up Rachel, on Christmas break from YWAM. The minute he spotted her, flagging him down in the pouring rain, his jitters evaporated. She was lovelier than ever with her dark hair caught in a yellow ribbon, flowing down to the middle of her back.

After lifting her suitcase into the trunk, he held an umbrella over her as she got into Lucio's Fiat. Brent immediately felt as comfortable with her as with a member of his own family. They chatted nonstop as if they'd never been separated, until arriving at the Giovanini wine estate.

He parked near the courtyard fountain, just as Alex and Jennalee zoomed in behind them on a scooter, splashing through a puddle before coming to a stop.

"*They* should've been the ones with the car," Brent said.

"They look so happy, I don't think they realize they're wet to the bone," said Rachel.

Alex pulled a manila envelope from under his jacket. "We're almost legal!" he shouted.

They looked so elated, Brent felt a pang of . . . well, not exactly jealousy. No, he sensed in his gut that even though it looked like things were coming together for them, there'd be trouble ahead. He sighed as they all went inside and kicked off their wet shoes.

Her hair dripping, Jennalee gave Rachel a wet hug. "I'm so glad you were able to come. All we need now is the registrar's official stamp and the official ceremony on Christmas Eve. Will you help me find a wedding dress this afternoon?"

"Better change your wet clothes," Alex said, "before Nonna attacks you with a towel and hot lemon tea."

"Here she comes!" Jennalee ran upstairs, laughing.

The speed of this marriage made Brent uneasy. He knew their parents would be stunned, maybe even outraged, by Jennalee's decision, but he couldn't put any blame on her. She was truly in love.

He saw Rachel peering at him.

"Is something wrong, Brent?" she asked. "You look so serious."

"I'll tell you later," he said. "Right now, I'm starved. Let's see what's in the kitchen."

What they found was a heaping platter of sandwich makings to be built on chewy Italian bread, with sharp cheeses and antipasti.

After lunch, when they felt so full they could barely move, Nonna asked the four of them for aid in finding something. Following her, they traipsed up a winding stone staircase to a tower attic room. Alex pulled a chain and a single low-watt light bulb snapped on. Boxes and trunks were piled in every corner, strung together with a few cobwebs.

"Gabe and I used to play hide and seek up here," said Alex.

Nonna, with a large skeleton key in her hand, strode up to an enormous wooden trunk, and dusted it off with her apron. She jiggled the key inside the lock until the curved lid came open. Kneeling beside it, she dug down with gnarled fingers and pulled out something white, tissue paper flying. It was a bridal gown.

"*Ecco qui, Alessandro,*" she said. "Your Mama's dress. Gina want your bride to have it."

"It's gorgeous," said Jennalee. She stroked it with her fingers. "Feels like pure silk."

"It's a great classic design. You've got to try it on," said Rachel. "Better than anything you'd find in the stores."

Nonna burst forth in Italian, fluctuating with her Sicilian dialect. Alex interpreted. "We'll go downstairs so Jenn can try it on. Nonna says she'll remake the dress however the bride wants it."

"I hope it fits so she won't have to," said Jennalee.

As they descended the spiral of stairs leading to the hall below, Rachel said, "We forgot the veil. I'll get it!" She went back up.

Soon, she caught up with them, grasping a length of white lace, and passed Brent and Alex. She went into Jennalee's bedroom and the door shut behind her.

Brent shuffled his feet in the wooden paneled hallway. Oohing and aweing echoed from the bedroom. This was boring.

He nudged Alex. "Let's go do something, this is awkward."

"I kind of wanted to see her in it," said Alex, with a shrug.

"She won't let you."

Nonna slipped out the door and hurried down the hall. From inside, Jennalee's voice commanded, "Alex, don't you dare come in; you can't see me in this dress until our wedding."

"See?" said Brent.

Pins in her mouth, Nonna came back, swinging a tape measure around her neck and mumbling, "My Gina, so tall. I fix it."

She went back into the room just as Rachel slipped out into the hallway. "It looks incredible on her, Alex. I'd help, only I can't sew."

She looked around, curiosity written all over her. "The Giovanini villa is enormous. And Brent said it's older than America. Can you show us around?"

"*Andiamo*," Alex said, "let's go!"

Brent thought he'd seen most of the mansion already, but after Rachel counted ten bedrooms, he said, "You've got more rooms than I thought. How many bathrooms?"

Alex smirked. "Three. There didn't used to be *any*, then my great-grandfather converted a few bedrooms."

They ended the tour outside in the wet, glistening courtyard, admiring the main balcony and portico, still dripping with rain.

Rachel breathed in and sighed. "It's the grandest house I've ever been in, much less stayed in."

"I'm glad you think so. Make yourself at home," said Alex, looking closely at Rachel's face.

Rachel studied him, too.

"You look familiar," she said. "Well, this *is* weird. Did you go to Faith Christian School in Portland around third grade?"

Alex clapped and pointed. "Yeah, third through fifth. So you're *that* Rachel Christenson?"

"Alex Campanaro! All this time I thought your last name was Giovanini."

"It's Mom's maiden name."

Rachel's mouth formed an O. Brent might as well have not been there as the two rattled on about their teachers, kids they knew, and Oregon. But he still listened closely, anxious to hear anything he could learn about Rachel's background.

"Good times," said Alex. "I loved Faith school. The teachers got me serious about serving God."

"Me, too," said Rachel. "We got real love from them, but did we ever have to toe the line!"

"Time-out," said Brent. "I get it you know each other. What I want to know is, did you *like* each other in grade school?"

Rachel rolled her eyes. "How should we answer him, Alex?"

"We were just friends," Alex said.

"Wait a minute," said Brent. "That's what everyone says." He pursed his lips.

"Bro, I mean it," said Alex. "You should've seen her in those days. She had some dorky looking glasses going on."

Rachel laughed. "True, I wear contacts now."

Alex said, "And she was way taller than any of us boys. Guess you shrunk, Rachel."

"Which is why you didn't recognize me right away, I suppose."

Alex nodded. "I guess we both look different, huh? Brent, what you need to know about Rachel is, even in grade school, she knew her Bible. And man, could she ever pray. You'd better 'up your game' if you want to get near her. She won't accept just any guy. It was hard to impress her then. I imagine it's worse now."

Rachel blushed a rosy color. "I'm going upstairs to check on Jennalee's dress."

"Didn't mean to embarrass you," Alex said. "C'mon, it's true and you know it."

She stopped on her way to the door and gave Brent a meaningful smile over her shoulder, which in his eyes, lit up the cloudy skies. Then she shook her long hair and went inside.

Even with the bright smile sent his way, a singular loneliness overcame Brent, almost as if he were dressed in his formal LDS missionary white shirt and tie, standing all alone in a huge field, far away from these born-again Christ-followers. Would he ever be one of them, or would Mormonism continue to cling to him?

Competitive adrenaline kicked in, and he asked, "Did every guy in your class like her?"

"Yeah, but no worries, Brent. Nothing we said or did ever impressed her. She wouldn't give us the time of day."

"So, what do you mean, 'up my game'?"

"I mean, dude, she's high up on the 'best girl ever' scale. Rachel was considered the 'cream of the crop' by her friends and teachers. I think she must be so far ahead with her experience of God that you've got to know your stuff. The only thing that might impress her is maturity in the Lord."

Brent's balloon of hope popped at Alex's remark. He hadn't known the truth of the biblical Jesus long at all. Why on earth would Rachel want to go out with *him*? Still, the smile she threw back at him must have meant she had a soft spot for him. There was one thing to do. Since he knew so little of the Bible, he'd start studying it every day. And maybe, just maybe, he'd stand a chance to gain something more than friendship.

Chapter Ten

Buried Treasure

The next morning, Alex came upon his uncle savoring a cup of dark roast in the kitchen. A sugar bowl sat nearby, and Uncle Lucio dropped a spoonful into his cup, then stirred with the same tiny spoon.

"*Buongiorno . . . momento*," he said, starting up the espresso machine. Within a minute, Uncle Lucio handed him a demitasse cup of thick coffee.

"Thanks, *Zio*, this should clear my head. I need to think sharp this morning."

"What bothers you, my boy?"

"Well, for one thing, Jennalee will be my wife in a few days."

His uncle laughed. "That bothers you? But that is not what you mean. A big responsibility, yes; bother, no."

Alex hesitated. "Right. I'm trying to think about the future. What's going to happen to our export business?"

"Ah, my son, while you were in hospital, Giuseppe and I and your mamma . . . we agreed to close the export side of the vineyard business. We did not realize how far the mafia had infiltrated, even in the north, where Giuseppe is. Up there, saboteurs destroyed a neighbor's vineyard by emptying their vats one night. Think of it, the whole year's harvest soaking into the ground, making puddles on the floor." Lucio closed his eyes and shook his head.

"Makes me sick to think about, Uncle."

"Italy's economy is not so good. And where money is to be made, the mafia are there. The poor would never join the mafia in good times, but now they work for them to feed their families."

Alex thought of poor, starved Fuglio. Maybe the boy's uncle, too, was forced by circumstances to join the mafia.

Lucio took a sip of his sweet coffee. "As your mother said, our export business 'wasn't meant to be.' Let's be happy now, my son. You're getting married soon. And we have new plans to improve our vineyard's production."

Alex breathed a sigh of relief but had another bothersome thought.

"What about the Maserati? Is insurance going to pay for it?"

"Not to worry, dear boy. The accursed *banditi* caused the wreck of our beautiful car. The insurance company is making payment. First we pay them . . . what is the word? Deductible."

Alex didn't want to ask but had to. "How much?"

"15,000 Euros. I know UniCredit Bank will give us the loan you signed for. You see? No need to worry."

His stomach dropped. There was no loan. He hadn't applied for it because that was the day he'd met Jennalee outside the Parthenon, and soon after, Firenza Tarentino stopped him outside the bank for what turned out to be more than a few minutes of small talk.

"Uncle, I hate to tell you this, but . . . the bank closed before I could sign for the loan. No excuses, but I thought I could go back the next day. Then, I couldn't because I got captured. I'm sorry."

Lucio stared at him. "The loan has not been applied for?"

Alex shook his head.

"It will be okay, my son. At least you're alive. You don't know how thankful I am to God you escaped death."

"Uncle," said Alex. "Somehow I'll pay for the deductible, I will. Should I go back and apply for the loan today?"

Uncle Lucio's tall frame sagged. "No, it's too late. I don't think they will give us a loan now. But we will find a way, son." Tight-lipped, he left the room.

What would they do?

All morning, the nagging problem followed him. Jennalee had gone shopping with Rachel for a few things she needed, and he was alone. Eventually, he found himself wandering outside in the vineyard where Brent was disposing of old grapevines.

He grinned at seeing Alex. "Hey bro, I know you're too weak to help." Then he saw Alex's face. "Hey, I'm kidding. Anything wrong?"

"The Maserati, that's what. I can't seem to forget it."

"It wasn't your fault, Alex, it just happened. I saw that car. Totaled, wasn't it?"

Alex bowed his head. "A horrible wreck." Bad situations clung to him like Joseph in the Bible. "What's awful is, I remember every second of that car's smash-up and then it rolling down the mountain." The movie in his brain played, along with the sound of the screeching metal.

"I bet there's a high deductible on a brand new Maserati Ghibli."

Alex winced. "Yep, 15,000 Euros. And because of me, we don't have the money."

Brent threw a bundle of vines into a utility trailer. "How's Lucio taking the loss of the Maserati?"

"He was pretty down this morning when I told him I didn't get a loan application signed before the wreck. Now he thinks they won't give it to us."

Brent didn't say anything and Alex drooped his head. Then, a sudden picture flashed into his mind. There was a maze of webs, and way down a tunnel, he saw . . . a treasure trove of bottles, under wooden tables. It was the valuable wine he'd found while in prison, hidden underground. If only he could retrieve them.

"Yeah, well . . . Lucio's such a good guy," said Brent. "Wish I could help."

"You can. There may be a way to get the money but I can't do it alone."

Brent put his rake aside and looked at him skeptically.

"My concussion caused me to forget about this, but I know where there's buried treasure." Alex felt himself smile for the first time that morning.

Brent's eyebrows shot up.

"You're looking at me like I'm crazy. Let me explain."

■   ■   ■

Buried treasure? Brent thought his brother-in-law's head injury must've gone pretty deep, but he saw that Alex was clearly excited by his idea.

"Let me explain. While I was locked up, I found a tunnel leading downhill. I could tell nobody had passed down it in years, because a wall of spiders' webs almost stopped me. I had to get a chair to knock them down."

Brent shuddered. "Sounds like a horror film. You should know something about me, Alex. I hate spiders."

Alex ignored him, though Brent didn't think it was on purpose.

"Anyway, at the end of the tunnel was a high cavern, about twelve feet to the ceiling. I could see because of an opening through the roof."

"I'm listening." Brent relaxed. What Alex said made sense so far.

"I found dozens of wine bottles under a wooden table. Someone had left it there to age, I guess, and forgotten about it. And the greedy *Camorra* wouldn't forget anything that valuable."

"Let's be practical, Alex," Brent said. "It's dangerous to go back to an aftershock area. I mean, they've had hundreds. Not to mention a mafia-controlled zone."

"I know, but I can't stop thinking about it. It's a waste of fine wine. And it's worth a lot. We can't tell Uncle Lucio because he'll forbid us to go look. He's overprotective. Treats me like his son."

Brent coughed, then said, "I've noticed that. But maybe he's right, Alex. Lucio says the mafia's in Taurasi, pushing for government contracts to rebuild. He's *really* scared of them now. Maybe we should be, too."

"But each bottle is worth hundreds, if not thousands of Euros, depending on its provenance."

"Meaning history? What if the history involves the mafia and they catch us?"

Alex shrugged. "I think they're too busy to care about small pickings like us. And a lot of them got killed in the quake."

"Okay, I'm from Utah, where most of us don't drink, and I'm not familiar with wine prices. Why is this wine so valuable?"

"It's made from the black Aglianico grape, arguably the fruit that started viniculture in Italy. The vines were brought from Greece before the birth of

Jesus. When aged, it's very expensive. I identified it by tasting it and figured out my location."

Brent couldn't help it; this intrigued him. "You did that just by tasting it? You're good, Alex. So . . . how many bottles are we talking about?"

"Dozens. To be fair, you should know it's hard to get to, maybe impossible."

Brent loved adventure. The more he listened, the more he wanted to go. He'd played opposing lawyer long enough. "Impossible you say? Hey, I'm your new brother-in-law. Let's make a stag party out of it. I mean, we won't drink it, just dig it out."

Alex laughed. "You're on. If it's completely buried, we'll let it rest in peace, but if we *can* get it out and sell it, I can pay the Maserati's deductible. What time is it?"

"About ten, are you thinking of going right away?"

"The sooner the better."

"Okay, on the way, can we pick up my motorbike in Castel di Sangro? As a plus, it's at a ski lodge with fantastic pizza."

Alex looked thoughtful. "Yeah, we'll go the long way then, because we might need it. It's about halfway to Taurasi."

A few yards away, Lucio started the engine of a four-wheeler and steered it towards them.

"He's coming, I'll help you get the rest of the vines into the trailer. I'm pretty sure he'll let us borrow the Giovanini Vineyard truck," Alex said. "The motorbike should fit in the back. Only, you might have to ride it when the truck's full of wine."

"Listen to the eternal optimist," Brent said. "Okay, let's do it, Lucio needs the money."

"I'll tell him about getting the scooter from Castel di Sangro and he'll let us go. And I'll tell him we have another errand, too."

After Alex explained, Lucio pondered the proposal, not asking at all about the other errand. "On one condition," he said, holding up his index finger, "you must return before the sun sets tomorrow. You have a wedding to get ready for."

"That's right," said Brent, remembering with a jolt. "Hey Alex, Jennalee and Rachel are coming down the driveway in the Fiat. You'd better tell the bride about this little trip by yourself, because I don't want to be around when you do. And I wouldn't mention anything about a stag party."

"Poor boy," Lucio added, watching Alex walk to the house. He winked at Brent. "He knows very little about women."

Chapter Eleven
Stolen Wine

"You drive," Brent told Alex, climbing into the passenger seat of the vineyard's truck.

"Okay, I feel way better now and believe me, I know the territory," Alex said.

"How did Jennalee take the news?"

"Uh . . . I promised to be back tomorrow, but she's not happy. You know I'd never leave her if we didn't have to do this for the money."

"What? Didn't she like your idea to get the payment for Lucio's car?"

"Well. . . I told her we were picking up wine. I didn't exactly say where. You know she wouldn't want us to go back into earthquake territory." Alex kept his eyes above the steering wheel. "I told her you have to get the motorbike, too."

"Did she ask to come with us?"

"No, but she can't anyway because she's supposed to pick up our license, and she and Rachel still have shopping to do for the reception."

"Interesting, Alex, because I told Rachel the whole truth. Jennalee should be finding out . . ." He looked at his phone. "About now."

Alex shrugged. "We're on our way, so what can she do? Hope she doesn't tell Lucio."

■　■　■

Brent shook awake on a sharp turn. He hadn't meant to drop off. "Sorry, Alex," he said, "guess I took a nap."

"You needed it. But I'm getting sleepy myself now," Alex said. "Talk to me, it helps."

"Well, come to think of it, there's a book I wanted to discuss with you," Brent said, stifling a yawn. "Jennalee told me you read *No Man Knows My History.*"

"Right, I read it last year. What do you want to know?"

"I want to know why the Missionary Training Center said to stay away from anyone who'd read that book. Basically, they told us the author's apostate and the book is from the devil."

Alex furrowed his brow. "Wow, they're a little defensive. They don't want anyone reading it probably because the evidence is hard to refute. See, the author was an historian who used original documents tracing Joseph Smith's life. With those sources, it's hard to deny what you are seeing; it's staring you in the face."

Brent wanted to know more. "Why were *you* interested in Joseph Smith? Most non-LDS know nothing about him."

Alex sped up to pass a truck. "Well, I didn't read it to bash Mormons. Not at all. At the time, I felt like I was falling in love with Jennalee and I had to know whether I should become LDS for her. And I found out why I couldn't."

"I didn't know you considered becoming LDS," Brent said.

"Yeah, I did, because you Saints are a great group of people with real moral values. I'd be stupid not to notice how much good you do. You help each other move, you give food to the poor, and lots more. I think sometimes Latter-day Saints are way better in the brotherly love department than a whole lot of evangelical Protestants."

"Nice to hear it." It was true that his people were good people.

"I had a strong desire to belong to your religion but I found out it stood completely on the claims of Joseph Smith and his visions. So I had to find out about him and the foundations of the Church."

Brent whistled under his breath. "Would you believe I did a similar search on Church history in the BYU Library? But I was less brave than you, I stopped my research at Joseph Smith's door."

Alex nodded. "I can see why. Red flags, I found lots of them. The title of the book is totally appropriate. Joseph Smith didn't want his history known. So, the author had to dig hard for sources from both inside and outside the Church. Newspapers, court records, books. And what she found . . . well, she managed to prove 'the Emperor had no clothes'."

Brent felt himself on edge, curious and disheartened at the same time. "Do you think I should read it?" He felt a stab of guilt when he said it.

"If you're at a place to examine Joseph Smith with a microscope, then yes."

Brent didn't know what to say. He paused, and said, "In my heart, I've already left a lot of my old beliefs. But I still don't know what to think about Joseph Smith. I'm starting to believe he's been photo-shopped into someone very different than who he really was."

"As an outside observer, that's how it looks to me," Alex said, as they sped by a stand of mountain pine trees.

"A few years ago, the Church finally admitted to the polygamy of Joseph Smith. He had like, thirty wives, some way younger than him. It grieved a lot of good people."

"I tell you, it's even hard to read about in *No Man Knows My History*. You can't help but question his true motives for marrying several women in a month. And a church that has those foundations is on shaky ground. I don't care that they don't believe in it now."

Brent looked out at the trees. "So if the 'Powers That Be' admitted the Prophet had extra wives, how can they say *No Man Knows My History* came from the devil? I've always had a pain in my gut about polygamy."

"Me, too. Think of sharing your father with fifty other kids."

Brent frowned. "Trouble is, I know God allowed it in the Old Testament and I don't understand why. . ."

Alex jumped in. "Even if polygamy is recorded in the Bible, it doesn't mean God approves of it. A lot of sin is recorded in the Bible. Look at Abraham. Unfortunate father of two nations that hate each other. And in Genesis, God made *one* helpmate and told Adam to cleave to her. Plural marriage is not intended by God."

Brent's trust of Alex went up a notch. The guy had really examined what he believed. He said, "You mentioned Adam and Eve. The LDS Genesis interpretation is way different than you evangelical Protestants believe."

"How?"

"We . . . I mean . . . Latter-day Saints put a positive spin on the fall of mankind. And we think Adam was the archangel Michael in the pre-terrestrial life. He helped create the world."

Alex's face looked perplexed. "You're really keeping me awake now. Anger tends to do that."

"Anger?"

"I get mad when I hear unbiblical doctrine. Brent, how can a man be an angel? And how can Adam, who was a *created* being, also create the world? It's all wrong."

"Well, I'm slowly discovering it's wrong, too, and now I have to work on straightening out the old narratives in my head."

"Whew," said Alex, "It would do a number on anyone. Brent, knowing what the Bible truly says is the most important thing. I'm trusting God to continue to show you, brother."

It was a relief to be called brother, but Brent still chafed a little. "Listen, I'm sensitive when non-Mormons criticize the Church, because without being raised LDS, it's hard to understand how it is."

Alex nodded. "Fair enough. You're right, I don't know how it is. But the author of the book on Joseph Smith *was* a Mormon. She found out so much, she couldn't go on believing."

"I'm sure it's a powerful book," said Brent, "I guess I should read it even if it upsets me."

"My opinion? It's true history, Brent, but give it a while. No need to read it yet. Let yourself soak in the *good* things in the Bible and true doctrine. You've read the book of John, right?"

"Absolutely, but I could read it a third time. John changed my life when I read it without my LDS opinions. I do have a few questions, though."

"Shoot," said Alex.

Much to Brent's joy, they talked about the Bible the whole rest of the way.

■ ■ ■

An hour later as they drove into Castel di Sangro, Brent gazed at the mountains and thought of the snowy Wasatch Front. His return to Utah wouldn't be long now. Religious mountains moved for him daily and he'd been *transformed* in a way he couldn't explain. There was no other word for it.

"Are you okay?" asked Alex, startling him.

"It's my old habit of staring into space. I'm thinking about Utah and what it will be like to live there now, after I've changed so much."

"I know what it's like for *me*," Alex said, with a wry smile. "And I'll help you out any way I can. Hey, here's the lodge. C'mon, let's get your scooter."

A member of the hotel staff unlocked the back shed where his motorbike was stored. With Alex's help, Brent rolled it into the back of the truck.

"I know it's ratty, but I paid a lot for it," Brent said, noticing Alex's color. "Hey, you've turned all white again."

"I guess I'm kind of worn out. Maybe I'm not as normal as I thought."

"We can spend the night here and get an early start tomorrow. I'll put the room on my card," Brent said.

"Good idea. Did you mention they have good pizza?"

■ ■ ■

The next morning, after shots of espresso, Brent and Alex climbed into the truck with renewed energy.

"I finally talked to Jenn while you were in the shower," said Alex, from the driver's seat.

"What'd she say? You know, besides her angry stuff?"

"She *was* kind of hysterical, mostly about my concussion."

"You mean she didn't ask 'What if there's another earthquake?'"

Alex suddenly looked grim. "I hear the aftershocks are almost over." He paused. "Maybe we shouldn't go through with it, Brent."

"Jennalee gave you cold feet."

"Maybe."

"You pray about everything, don't you? Did you pray about this?"

Alex stared at the road ahead. "No, I started planning on my own. I should know better. We need to pray."

"Here?"

Alex had already started. "Lord God, Almighty King, I assumed I knew your will. Help me to discern whether or not to go forward with our plan. I'm sorry I've been caught up in my own purposes and presumed you would be, too. We can't do this without you, so, Master, show us a path if there is one. Make a way for us if you want us to proceed."

The unpretentious prayer touched Brent. Alex came to God just as he was, a mere human.

"And thanks for this new brother-in-law of mine."

"Amen." Brent said.

"Now we'll trust God to open doors or close them."

"Right," said Brent, wondering how Alex knew what an open door was. A question kept coming up in his brain. "About this wine. Who *does* it belong to? I mean, I know it's old, but there's got to be an owner."

"There may be a label, and that will tell us who it belongs to. The bottle I tried didn't have one. Or maybe I didn't see it."

"You remember I hate spiders, so which one of us goes below ground first?"

He liked Alex's chuckle. "We'll flip a coin."

"There's another problem," said Brent. "The criminal underworld might be uptight about us finding something valuable right under their noses. It's a terrible thing to annoy the mafia."

Alex squinted at the rising sun and flipped down the visor. "Our plan is to get the wine out before they even know about it. I assume at least part of their spy network was ruined by the quake."

"So if we can't find it, nobody will ever know, right? And if we do find it, it's ours."

Alex's face lit up. "I'm surprised to hear that from a lawyer-type like yourself."

Brent laughed. "Well, yeah, but in my experience, real thieves don't pray before they take the loot. I agree with you. If it's labelled, we give it to the owner. It's all good."

Alex ran his fingers through his hair. "I have a feeling we won't be the first to take this wine."

Chapter Twelve

The Underworld

On the back of Brent's motorbike, Alex squeezed his eyes shut at the sight of the hilltop where he was held in prison. The sharp pain of his ordeal a mere month ago jabbed at him. His head wound had healed, but inside, he would never forget. Why had he come here to face the scenes of destruction again?

The scooter bumped over a goatherd's path, and he gripped Brent's shoulders as grass tussocks nearly bounced him off. They passed Taurasi. The sight of the village's tragic emptiness saddened him. One church's bell tower had mostly caved in and its medieval dome looked like a cracked egg. But the bells were still in place, exposed by fallen bricks.

Finally, Brent halted the scooter at the craggy top of the hill near a crop of boulders and they hopped off. When the kick stand sunk into the soft earth, they laid the bike down in the grass.

"You can't be serious. You were caged up *here?*" Brent shook his head. "One of the refugees told us the castle was a thousand years old and fell in this earthquake. I knew you'd been through a lot, Alex, but you could've been buried."

"It's the grace of God I wasn't. My jail cell is under those stones."

"Unbelievable." Brent spread out his arms. "Where do we start?"

Alex pointed to the pile of rocks ahead and willed himself to focus on the goal. Hadn't God shown him the wine for a reason? It would help make things right. Choking down fear, Alex marched towards the ruined fortress like a soldier going into battle.

He turned to Brent. "If we trace my steps from the underground jail in the direction of the tunnel, we can come up with a trajectory. See the cliff? My window looked out from it. The tunnel led away from the cliff at about a 45-degree angle. We could use trigonometry to figure it out."

Brent groaned. "Trig? You sound like one of those Accelerated Placement students."

"I was a real geek, I know. Truth is, I don't like trig much and I thought *you* might be able to figure this out. But . . . the other way is to guess."

"That would be my way."

"Okay, here's an educated guess." Alex started taking large steps toward the ruins. "Lombard castles had courtyards. And see how the stones fell outward instead of inward?"

Brent's voice sounded excited. "So, if we're lucky, the courtyard is behind the fallen walls and is still an open space. My guess is the wine cave is under the courtyard."

"I agree."

Alex clambered up the fallen wall and Brent climbed up beside him. He saw what he'd suspected. "It's a grassy square, wide open. It's about twenty yards angled away from the cliff. I think we guessed right."

Alex found it harder to climb down on the other side. And the logistics in his head told him that even if they managed to get the wine out, there would be no easy way to carry it over the fallen walls and cart it down the hillside. It took ten minutes of scraped hands and knees, but once into the courtyard, they strode across the lumpy grass, looking for clues.

Brent shouted, "Hey, look here! There's a crater, like an underground . . . *whoa!*"

Alex looked up in time to see Brent sink into the ground in a puff of white dust. He ran to the spot and clawed at the manhole-sized cave-in, trying not to fall in himself. Then he heard a faint call from below.

"I'm okay! Ow . . . ow."

"I'm coming down, Brent!" he yelled. Scrambling through his knapsack, he found a rope and tied it to a half-broken stone pillar.

He looped the rope in his hands and propelled down through the hole, landing on his feet. It relieved him to see Brent upright, hobbling towards him with a dusty white face. Alex got out his flashlight and shined it on the inner walls of a large domed cavern.

"Guess that's God's open door. I think you prayed for that," Brent said, laughing.

He laughed, too. "I had no clue it would be a hole in the ground."

"We didn't even have to flip a coin. I got down here with the spiders first," Brent said, rubbing his leg near his shoe. "But I twisted my ankle."

Alex pointed his flashlight to the ankle. "Hm. Swelling up pretty good, isn't it?"

"It's not so bad," said Brent, taking his sock off. "But I'll be a gimpy groomsman at your wedding."

Alex pressed on Brent's ankle bones. "Don't think anything's broken, but when we get back we need a doctor to make sure."

"Hey, now that I look around, I see zero cobwebs," said Brent. "The earthquake must have cleaned the spiders out."

"That ought to make you happy."

Brent sat on a pile of rubble and shone his phone light on the walls. "Which way to the treasure?"

"The wine should be about here, under . . . wait, Brent! See the wooden tables?"

Alex stumbled over some rocks on his way there, and reached the table with a bruised knee. "Here it is! The bottle I opened. It's the best Taurasi wine ever," he said, pulling out the crumbly cork. But sipping it again wasn't quite the same. His taste buds didn't catch the deliciousness. *Strange.*

Brent hobbled around the rocks. "Hey, I think I see a label on one of the bottles. And there are letters stenciled on the crates."

Alex blew the dust off as Brent shone his light on the crate. Faded words melted into the background when they saw a large black swastika.

"Whoa. Alex, this is Nazi wine."

The thought of who had hidden the wine made the hair rise on Alex's neck.

"German soldiers must've stashed it here to retrieve after the war," said

Brent. "Lucky for us, they never came back for it. Well, we can't give it back to Nazis. They're all in Argentina."

Alex stared at him. "You mean that?"

"Yeah. I should know, I spent two years there. A lot of Nazis escaped from the Allies and went on with their lives in South America."

"That's rotten," said Alex. He glanced at the labeled bottle with a sinking feeling inside. "We'd better read this label and find out where it's from."

Brent nodded and shone his light on it.

Alex squinted and read the words, "Bernardino Vineyards." He swallowed. "Ah . . . the Bernardinos. I know of them. They're still the best producers in Campania."

"Wow," said Brent. "So the family who produced this wine is alive and well, and . . . we have to return it to them."

"Yes," Alex said, "we have to do the right thing." He'd have to think of another way to get the money for the Maserati.

Hiding his disappointment, he knelt and dusted off the thick wooden case holding the other bottles. "Look at what this says," he said, pointing to the rough wood. Alex tried his best German accent. "Panzer-Division 1. Hermann Göring. Generalmajor Wilhelm Schmalz, 1944."

"Marked for Hermann Göring," Brent said. "I saw a documentary about him; he was the head of the Third Reich's Air Force. The guy loved the high life; especially wine."

An odd bit of dust drifted down on them from the ceiling above. Suddenly, their flashlights swerved as the ground heaved with a huge jolt. Alex staggered to balance himself as fear punched him in the gut.

"Under the tables! Quick!" Brent said.

There was just enough room to slip under the oaken tables that sheltered the wine crates. If only they were up on top of the ground instead of under it. . . Alex held his breath, and in a few harrowing seconds, the aftershock halted.

"Wow. A bad aftershock a whole month later," said Brent, getting up and dusting off his hair. "It didn't last long but oh, my heck, I hated the big jolt at the start. Need help?" He extended his hand to Alex.

But Alex was frozen in place.

"I can't get up," he said, embarrassed by his shaky voice.

"Take it slow," said Brent. "I'll wait for you."

Was this what a panic attack felt like? Alex told himself to breathe, but his lungs didn't want to expand. He coughed, breathed big, and stretched his right leg out, then the other, until he stood beside Brent, who steadied him with his arm.

"No wonder you froze, after what you've been through. Scared me, too."

"Yeah, thanks. I don't know what happened. I just couldn't move." Alex took another deep breath and somehow, the fear subsided. "It's time to get out, before a stronger one hits."

"Yeah, this so-called roof could cave."

"Grab a few bottles and take them with us," Alex said, reaching into the crates and setting about six bottles up on the table. "We'll tell the Bernardinos where to retrieve them. It's the only way. We can't move them over that fallen wall. They'll have more help."

"How many bottles are there altogether?" Brent asked, as he got ready to climb up the rope, with two bottles stuffed into his cargo jeans, and some in his backpack.

"Twelve bottles in twelve crates makes 144, minus the one I tasted from."

"Hey, bring that one here and we'll finish it off. This is your stag party, you know." Brent let out a hearty laugh, making Alex relax again.

"Brent, you and I are way too busy to get drunk. Not that we would anyway. Wine tasters don't work like that."

"How do you taste so much wine without getting buzzed?"

"We spit it out and rinse our mouths. Otherwise, we couldn't discern the nuances of each one. We can taste for hours and it doesn't affect us."

Brent looked incredulous. "You spit it out? Gross."

"I don't think anything of it. But don't worry, I'll bring that bottle so Bernardinos can taste it."

"Well," said Brent, "I wouldn't want to be responsible for a drunken stag party anyway. My sister does have a teeny bit of a temper."

"I love her, temper and all," Alex said, feeling calmer thinking about

Jennalee. "Let's go home. The rats are getting curious by now." He tried to hide his grin.

"Rats? In that case, we're not necessarily in this together," Brent said, "because I'm out of here."

"So, it's not just spiders you're afraid of?"

"*Andiamo*, as you say."

Alex had to admire how Brent kicked off the cavern wall with his good foot and climbed up hand over hand. Then he shimmied through the opening, and in a minute, dangled the rope down for Alex.

"You're next!" he shouted.

He hurried to put several bottles inside his pack and shouldered it. Fumbling to climb up the rope, Alex's claustrophobia surged back. He took a long breath. Keep looking up, he told himself. Paul, who was lowered into Mamertine Prison's hole survived despair by looking up.

And almost to the top, Alex knew that his big God had resurrected him from this same underground pit in the past, and would save him now, too.

After Brent pulled him up through the manhole, he said, "You're about as pale as a tanned Italian gets. You don't like it down there, do you? And something tells me it's not just the rats and spiders."

Chapter Thirteen

Disappointment

"They'll be back," Rachel assured Jennalee. "From what I know of your brother, he's a responsible guy. Alex is, too."

Jennalee sniffed back her worries. "Alex doesn't know the license isn't approved. I can't even text him about it. From what you told me, they're in a dead cell phone area."

When Jennalee related the bureaucratic dilemma to Nonna, the grand old lady, in a feisty mood, took her to the mayor's office to complain. They talked to everyone there, only getting shrugs and frowns for answers. Despite Nonna's arguing, they were forced to return to the villa without an official stamp or legal license. No one except the mayor could finalize it and someone finally said he was out on a family emergency and wouldn't be back for days.

"I thought he was a bachelor, Nonna. Where's his family?" said Jennalee.

"*Tutti noi abbiamo una Mamma,*" she said.

Yes, everyone has a mother, she thought. But when Alex's grandmother couldn't get it done, discouragement filled Jennalee's soul. Christmas was in three days, and she and Brent had to fly home that day.

Back at the villa, she started to pack her clothes as Rachel watched.

"I don't understand," said Jennalee. "There's been so much prayer about this wedding."

"Sometimes God opens a door and shuts a window," her friend said, "or is it the other way around? Anyway, I know you two will marry, whether here or in America. It'll happen, Jennalee. You have a true dedication to each other that few couples have."

"Thanks. No matter where we end up, will you be my maid of honor?"

Rachel nodded emphatically. "I would love to come alongside you on that day."

The sound of an old-fashioned doorbell interrupted them. Rapid Italian streamed through the foyer and the women rushed downstairs to see what was happening.

"Surprise!" said Alex's mom from under the arm of her own mother, who held both Gina and her son Gabe firmly in a hug, kissing them.

Freeing herself, Gina said, "We flew in as soon as we could. A son only gets married once. Hopefully, anyway. We wouldn't miss it for anything. And it's Christmas besides."

Alex's brother Gabe yawned. "Mom, I'm going upstairs to a nice warm bed," he said. "I couldn't sleep much on the plane. Nice to see you, Jennalee and . . ."

"This is my friend Rachel," said Jennalee.

Gabe shook her hand.

"Nice to meet you, Rachel," Gina said, looking a little past her. "Where's Alex?"

Nonna looked suddenly serious. She took Gina by the arm, and led her into the kitchen, whispering. Jennalee and Rachel peeked around the corner as the conversation got louder until it reached a crescendo, and Nonna and Gina waved their arms in a frenzy.

When the girls finally got the courage to go in, Gina was sipping a cup of tea. A fresh slice of Nonna's crusty rustic bread, baked in an ancient brick oven was beside her.

"*Mamma mia!*" she said, noticing their venture into the room. "I'm trying to calm myself. Nonna told me about the wedding troubles. Have some tea and stay a while. . . I didn't catch your last name, Rachel."

"Christianson. I'm a friend of Jennalee's brother."

Gina's smile widened. "I remember you, honey," she said, getting up to hug Rachel. "You went to Faith Christian School with Alex! How on earth did you land here in Italy?"

"I'm with Youth with a Mission. And I met Jennalee's brother in Argentina. We were both on missions there." Rachel blushed a little.

"What a small world. I mean, what are the odds? Surely Alex recognized you?"

"Yes, he did," said Rachel, "it's strange, isn't it? And I'm excited, Mrs. Campanaro, because Jennalee's just asked me to be her maid of honor."

"Whenever we get married, that is," said Jennalee.

"Call me Gina now, Rachel. I'm not your substitute teacher any more. Girls, I wish we could get through the red tape here in Italy, but we may have to accept the slowness of Italian bureaucrats. My mother tried, though, didn't she?" Gina glanced at the aproned back of her petite mother at the sink. "Speaking of slow, I can feel jetlag creeping up on me. Did you say where Alex was?"

Jennalee let out an extra-large sigh. "We haven't told you yet. He went to get some wine he found while he was captured."

"What? Another crazy adventure? And he left you behind?"

"My brother Brent went with him, while I stayed to deal with this wedding paperwork."

"Men! We'll have to make some plans while they're gone," Alex's mother said. "While the cat's away. . ."

Rachel giggled. "You always used to say the same thing when you were our substitute teacher."

"Yes, but I meant it in a good way."

"I totally remember. When our teacher came back and saw our spotless desks and the boards all cleaned, she was so happy. We even put the books in order on the shelves."

"So, by God's grace, we have to try to set this right, don't we?" said Gina. "Even if there are obstacles, we'll push through them. When you don't have an agenda and set up a schedule, nothing happens."

Jennalee admired how Gina had taken gentle command.

"Tomorrow, our plan B will begin," said Gina. "I'd like to stay up longer, but sleepy time tea is starting to hit."

■ ■ ■

By mid-morning of the next day, the three women had chosen the time, place, and caterer for the wedding in Utah. Using the internet, Jennalee found a florist, a baker, and even a wedding coordinator skilled in smoothing family differences. She chose her talented mother, Marjorie, to coordinate the music along with formal clothes for Jennalee's brothers and the other groomsmen.

"The Christmas Eve wedding will be transformed into an engagement celebration," said Gina. "No need to change the invites or the fancy meal Nonna has planned."

What an encouragement to Jennalee's soul! And there was nothing like Rachel's bright personality to cheer a person up.

"You brought my hope back," she told them. "I feel bonded to you both after this. Would you believe I'm afraid to tell my own mother about our engagement?"

"Why haven't you told her?" asked Gina.

"Rejection, I guess. And, to be truthful, I'm scared of waffling to please my parents. There's a lot of pressure to conform in Utah as you know. What I most fear is that they'll hurt Alex by not accepting him. They may insist he becomes LDS to marry me."

"People are afraid of anything that forces change." Gina beamed at her. "Love them anyway." She suddenly looked slightly worried. "Have you heard from Alex yet?"

"He finally texted from another area and explained why he's late. An acceptable excuse so far, but I'll let him tell you the rest of the details when he gets here."

Gina sighed. "I won't worry then. Girls, this is going to be one fabulous wedding. God is going to make a way. A quick prayer. . ."

Her prayer was simple and direct to a personal God.

Jennalee felt joyful again. With the planned event in Utah firm in her mind, her disappointment at not getting married in Italy felt less painful. And when her parents realized the wedding would take place on the first Saturday in May, they'd have to bless it, wouldn't they? Her father would walk her down the aisle. At least, that was the plan.

■　　■　　■

Before dinner, she and Rachel talked in Rachel's room.

"Judy from YWAM told me Italians dress formally for Christmas, so I brought every nice dress I had with me," said Rachel. "Want to borrow one?"

Jennalee pointed at her large suitcase. "I assume they're in there."

"Wait till you see. Pick any one you want." Rachel opened it, bringing out a white sleeveless dress with pearls sewn on a red satin neckline. "Like this one?"

"That's a knock-out Christmas dress," Jennalee said, "but I can't imagine myself in it."

Rachel looked at her, then at the dress. "A little pale for you, but there are three more." On the bed she laid out three choices: a soft lavender one, a deep electric blue, and an emerald dress with gold netting.

Rachel held up the velvety green fabric against Jennalee's face. "This color looks great on you."

Jennalee chafed at making a decision. "There's one problem. They're all sleeveless."

Rachel looked puzzled.

"I don't know how to explain this," said Jennalee, "or how much you know, but I'm still wearing my LDS undergarments. I haven't yet decided what to do about them."

Rachel looked a little panicked. "Oh, I always thought your brother wore an awfully thick undershirt. So you're talking about some kind of ceremonial underwear, right?"

Jennalee swallowed hard. Non-Latter-Day Saints never understood. "Right, well, sort of. We wear sacred undergarments given to us in the temple after the covenants we agree to, and it's a reminder of our promises to God. We can't go sleeveless. The white dress is gorgeous but it's too short at the knee for the same reason. It wouldn't cover my garment."

Rachel slapped her hand to her mouth. "I'm sorry," she said, as if she'd offended Jennalee.

Jennalee shook her head and smiled. "Don't be. How could you know? Besides, maybe I'll take a bold step and discard it like Brent did."

Rachel colored rosy pink. "Is it the same thing as wearing a cross?"

"Sort of, but garments bind you to the LDS temple." Jennalee paused. "Come to think of it, I wear a cross, not because of any church, but to remind me of Jesus and represent him to the world."

"There's a huge difference then."

"Yes. My main problem is, I gave up normal underwear for the rest of my life, so I don't have anything except my bras. We wear those on top of the undergarments."

Rachel's face looked horrified. "You do?" She winced, saying, "Listen, I just bought some brand-new underthings. They still have the tags. You can try them on. Totally up to you. Don't do anything against your conscience."

"I'll think about it," Jennalee said, sounding weaker than she felt. She wished she could've passed it by Brent, but he was still gone.

Just because her garments itched and sagged, should she give them up? She'd begun to resent them, but that wasn't enough of a reason. Vaguely, she remembered the old story about being in physical danger if she didn't wear them.

Could it be true? She thought not. Her new life centered on Jesus, not sacred clothing, not covenants given in a temple before she knew Jesus himself. Her complete trust would have to be in the Good Shepherd of her life, not this underwear.

"Wish I could help," said Rachel. "Maybe we could pin your long underwear back and up a little?"

Jennalee laughed. "Thanks, Rachel, but if your new underthings fit me, I'm going to go with green dress."

She took the lingerie Rachel gave her and disappeared into her room next door. It felt good to peel off the undergarments that had encumbered her by their heaviness, and put on the light, airy pieces Rachel had given her. But she folded the garments respectfully and put them in her suitcase. Then she slipped the green dress on. Opening the door, she went out to show Rachel.

"That's the one," said Rachel with joy in her voice. "Brings out your hair and eyes."

"You don't know what a help you are in taking this step, Rachel. I'm free and I won't go back. I jumped over the edge into complete faith in Jesus.

Maybe that's how marriage feels . . . like leaping over a cliff."

"You and Alex are two of the bravest people I know, Jennalee. Might as well jump."

She'd need more courage, because in a mere four months, she and Alex would exchange forever vows in front of a living God for their lifetimes on this earth. Earth would have to be good enough because heaven was reserved for Jesus, who'd said there was no marriage in heaven. And she believed his words.

Chapter Fourteen

The Luxury of Hate

Alex took four wine bottles from his backpack and placed them on the Bernardinos' dining table, where members of the family stood in awe, staring at them. They laughed and cried, phoned others to come and see, all in rapid Italian.

Over the noise of a generator outside, Alex said to Brent, "I don't think we'll be able to go home tonight." This tribe was determined to show them appreciation, and in Italy, that meant a major celebration.

But Alex longed to get back. Pleading texts appeared on his phone from Jennalee that she'd sent earlier in the day. He'd answer as soon as he could.

"*Grazie, gentiluomini.*" The family patriarch greeted them, enveloping Alex and Brent with manly kisses. "This wine was lost forever. Now you Americans bring us a miracle the same as when you free us from Hitler's army. I send my sons tomorrow so you can show them the place where is the other bottles."

"*Signore,*" said Alex, "we must go home tomorrow, so we drew a map of where the wine is. With coordinates. You'll need plenty of rope and several people to carry it out. And there may be aftershocks. You must be very careful."

The big man nodded. "*Si,* is good. Tonight, you stay in our guest house. Our wine cellars in Taurasi were crushed by the *terremoto,* but in this new modern house, we have small damage and none of our family was killed. Now we have a generator for power."

His son, a man of about forty, said in English, "Tonight, dinner and a toast! Such good and honest men are rare."

"*Grazie*," said Alex, "for dinner and the offer of your guest house."

He and Brent would have to see this through. He sneaked a quick text to Jennalee that he'd explain more when he got back.

When he looked up, a wizened old woman dressed in black had entered the room. The crowd hushed. Alex perceived a nobleness around her, as she approached him and Brent with tears on her wrinkled cheeks.

"This is my Aunt Liliana," said *Signore* Bernardino. "She wishes to tell you about the stolen wine."

The old woman bowed to Brent and Alex as though they were dignitaries. The family gathered around to hear a story they'd no doubt heard many times, with her nephew interpreting for them.

"We have just survived a terrible earthquake," Aunt Liliana said, "But it is not the worst thing that has happened to our family. You cannot know how much it means to have our wine back. The night it was taken . . . is forever burned in me."

The old lady paused and swallowed hard. "The year was 1943 and the harvest was one of the best we'd ever had. *Eccelente!*" She kissed her closed fingers and released them. "We work hard for that harvest. But I never forget the Nazi General who pounded on our door that night pretending to buy wine. He wore shiny knee boots and at his neck, a fat cross. His Panzer tanks surrounded our vineyard. His name was Wilhelm Schmalz."

Brent whispered, "That's the name stamped on the crates."

Aunt Liliana didn't hear him. "Papa showed them our cellars. The Nazi General threw a few lire at us and commanded his men to pack crate after crate of the best we had." She paused. "And then they took Papa."

She looked at each face of her relatives. "We never saw our father again. Later we heard they burned the house next door with our neighbors inside. Our whole village was burned! I have worn black ever since, to mourn Papa and the others who died that night."

Alex told her how sorry he was; Brent did the same.

"*Si, grazie,*" she said. "A year later, this Nazi General was captured by the Americans. It ate my heart away that he was only locked up for five years. But God helped me forgive Schmalz."

Scowling, Brent asked, "How could you forgive such a horrible man?"

Her nephew relayed the question.

"You ask how? After I come back to live on this estate after the death of my husband, I saw into my heart. I realized . . . under certain circumstances, I could be as horrible as a Nazi. Yes, my heart was hard from holding bitter hate in it for such a long time. Evil grows."

Her sadness dissipated and she smiled with an angelic calm, resembling a Raphael Madonna.

"God in his grace showed me I would miss heaven with this unforgiving inside. I don't want to miss heaven. To never again see my Papa or my husband? Or Jesus? Nothing is worth missing Paradise. No, we cannot allow ourselves to have the luxury of hate."

The story pinged off of Alex's heart like a pebble on a hubcap. He had some forgiving to do. The Putifaros and their cruel mafia friends; he'd almost died because of them. And there were the high school students in Utah who'd shunned him.

Alex looked at his shoes. Most of all, he needed to forgive Jennalee's parents for trying to keep her away from him. But he couldn't do it here, not now.

Liliana gazed around the room at her family and guests. "It's time to take off the rags of mourning. Now I can wear bright colors in celebration of the return of the wine by these Americans! It is a sign I forgive the Nazis."

There was toasting, along with a delicious dinner. Alex kept a friendly face through it all. Afterwards, he told them he needed some air and walked outside to the front of the large house where the night wind licked at his longish hair. He'd need a haircut before the wedding.

He started to pray, but the presence of the Lord eluded him. It would be so much easier to put the forgiveness stuff on hold. . .

Feeling alone, he tried Facetime but it didn't work, and his calls didn't go through, so he texted Jennalee.

Sorry, Jenn, I'll tell you the story when I get there tomorrow. Short version is we returned the wine to the people who made it. They are celebrating with us.

She texted back. *I'm glad you're okay.*

Alex spoke his text. *You should see your brother. He's living it up.*

Her text came quick on top of his. *Problems here. Our license isn't signed by mayor. Family emergency and no one can find him.*

He texted back furiously. *You're kidding, right? Cancelled?*

It took a full minute to receive a reply. *Not cancelled. Changed to an engagement party.*

So, they had to wait. Again. He knew Jennalee would be rattled by this. He texted: *It will be okay. I will be there soon. I love you.*

She sent a heart emoji back.

No wedding haircut was needed now; he'd let it grow. And Italy's slow bureaucracy wouldn't stop the wedding momentum, only change the focus. They'd get married the right way, in Utah. No eloping, no running away from problems, even though it was a sore temptation. They'd have to face the strong disapproval of Jennalee's family sometime, and whatever happened, he'd have to forgive them.

Chapter Fifteen

Keep Walking

"Wake up, Brent! After your long nap, we're back," said Alex.

After an early morning send-off by the Bernardinos, Brent and Alex drove back to Rome, and arrived at the villa before lunch time. It surprised Brent how pleased he was to see the place. Almost like coming home.

"And not one, but two women welcome us," Brent said, catching sight of Jennalee and Rachel in the courtyard ahead. "It's like we're Odysseus' men, returning from war." He thumped his chest in a mock Roman salute.

"It *was* sort of a war," said Alex, "and you're wounded. You need a doctor to look at your ankle."

"Didn't I tell you? Last night, one of the uh . . . Bernardino girls iced it and made me drink some absolutely terrible firewater. I slept like a baby, like I'd never twisted it."

Alex laughed. "*Grappa*'s good medicine, but it's an acquired taste. I'll bet you're hurting now, though."

Brent grunted a 'Yes', but he didn't want to waste time seeing a doctor, not after catching sight of Rachel. As she approached the car, the hurting in his ankle was the least of his concerns.

Alex rushed out of the car and Brent thought he and Jennalee would never end their long hug. As he got out, the weight on his ankle gave way and he stumbled a bit, and it was a good thing Rachel didn't notice. She went on chatting about happenings at the villa while he was gone.

From the balcony came a cry of 'Surprise!' and he saw Alex look up and wave. The engaged couple charged up the balcony stairs where Alex bear-hugged a well-dressed woman and swung her in circles. The woman cried out in mock protest. Laughing, they all went inside.

"Alex's mom and brother came in on a late flight," said Rachel. "For the wedding."

"I thought so. Nice of them to come," said Brent, "but Alex told me it's been changed to an engagement party. I imagine Jennalee's disappointed. He drove like a crazy man to get here; those two can't be separated for long."

"Jennalee was really upset, but the party will be a magnificent Italian feast for family and friends, as I understand it; Alex's grandmother is making roast pork, several risottos, and swordfish as only a Sicilian can."

Rachel led him by the elbow through the gate to the back veranda and kept talking.

"We can meet up with Alex's family later, Brent. You'll love them. But right now I want to hear about your whole adventure." She stopped short and stared at his lame foot. "Wait a minute, why are you limping?"

■   ■   ■

"I told you it doesn't hurt that bad," Brent shouted into the kitchen from a couch in the sitting room. His ankle throbbed mercilessly, but he didn't care.

Rachel came back from the kitchen with an ice bag. "If it doesn't hurt much, why are you hobbling? Put your foot up on the ottoman," she said with authority, tucking the cold bag around his ankle. "Look at the bruising all the way to your knee. I hope you didn't break it, Brent."

"Sometimes a sprain is worse than a break." He frowned. "Alex checked it, but says I need a doctor to make sure nothing's broken."

"Ibuprofen?" she asked, holding out two pills and a glass of water.

"Sure, only I've discovered a better painkiller called *Grappa*. You wouldn't have any of that, would you?" When she shook her head with a quizzical look, he took the pills and drank them down.

"So, how's my sister *really* doing about not getting married?" he asked.

With a hint of a smile, she said, "Nonna tried to get the Italian bureaucracy to move faster, but couldn't. And Jennalee cried a lot, so we prayed together. Now she's doing better than you might think." Rachel's face lit up. "Best of all, Alex's mom and I helped her plan the entire wedding in Utah. We've set the date, texted the pastor, ordered the flowers, everything. She'll take Gina's dress with her and they'll be married in May. Since your mother's a music person, she'll be in charge of songs and a few other things."

"You did all that while we were gone?" He paused. "You did know that my parents are against the match? I guess we'll see what happens when we get back."

"Tell me what your family's like, Brent."

He took a deep breath. "My dad's an LDS Stake President; which means he's pretty high up in the Church. On the outside, my dad is perfect in every way. I have a stay-at-home mom who keeps schedules running smooth with my four younger brothers. I'm close to Mom, and she really is kind of a musical genius. She's always been an encourager, except when things threaten her LDS life. I try to help her out when Dad's gone for business. He's in land development."

"Sounds like any family, only way more kids." She sat down on the ottoman and in the sunlight from the window, her dark hair glinted a tiny bit of red.

Brent took a deep breath. "I've been wanting to thank you for your prayers . . . after I got back from my mission and had to face my parents about my new faith."

"I was glad to pray, Brent. I sort of wished . . . I could have been with you during that time."

Heat crept up Brent's face. "Well, I made it through with God's strength. Now comes the biggest challenge. That would be trying to adjust to Utah with new beliefs. On top of that, I want to help Ammon with his father's case."

"How *is* Elder Carr?" she asked.

"To tell the truth, depressed. So much has happened to him since he got home. Ammon's dream was to go to college, not take his father's job in a coal mine to pay bills. When his dad woke from the coma and told me he was pushed on purpose, I figured Ammon needed lawyers."

"How involved are you going to be?"

"I'm counting on my uncle and cousin to take the case. I'm years away from graduating from law school, but I'd like to be in the courtroom for Ammon's sake."

"Poor Ammon, such a good soul."

"He is, isn't he?"

"While you're gone, I'll be doing Youth with a Mission for a couple more months."

"Then what?" asked Brent.

"I'll go back to live with Alison in Portland. You remember her?"

"Yes, she was with you in Argentina; Ammon kind of liked her."

"Well, poor Alison's pursuing a guy who doesn't give her the time of day. Plus, she's going to nursing school. I might try to be a nurse, too."

"Sounds good." Brent bluffed confidence in the face of their separation. "You'll make a good nurse. Look, you're already practicing on me."

She tilted her head. "The thing is, I'm not too sure about my future. How long are you going to be with Ammon?"

"As long as the case takes. To tell the truth, Ammon's in shock I'm no longer LDS. He doesn't trust non-Mormons, but I'm his friend and I won't abandon him no matter what."

Her eyes brightened. "He's a sweet guy, but I knew he didn't understand what Alison and I talked to you about. It can be a huge risk telling people the *true* Gospel. For some people it takes a long time to understand. They get confused."

Brent locked his gaze on her. "I might as well tell you that you messed with our minds, Rachel. For me, anger came out. I must've been in the first stage of examining what I really believed. I had to learn to think differently about everything I'd been taught since I was little."

In a near whisper she said, "Jesus *compelled* me to tell you what I knew to be true."

"Through it all, Rachel, you don't know how grateful I am that you took the risk. God was revealing himself to me for a long time. Nudging me, but I kept fighting. I used to make fun of you evangelical Christians. I thought you had a religion just like I did, but mine was better."

"You *were* kind of a hard-core religious guy when we first met," said Rachel.

"Kind of? With the Holy Spirit turning me inside out, I got testy. It wasn't *you*, it was your God I wrestled with. Remember how you told me to pray for understanding when I checked out the things you said were in the Bible? Well, whenever I'd look at the whole chapter with open eyes, there it was, in black and white."

Rachel blushed a rose color which made her even prettier. "When you told me about the night you called out to God and he showed you who he truly is, I was overjoyed, Brent. You have to believe that peace will follow you to Utah, no matter what happens. In Philippians, it says, 'He who began a good work in you, will carry it on to completion.'"

"I believe that. Mine wasn't a lightning bolt experience, but the next day everything seemed right in the world, you know? And that feeling grew, until colors were brighter and the world was sharpened like a 3-D picture. I started to love everybody, but I knew it wasn't me loving them, it was God's love. Now *everything's* new; my attitude, my beliefs, my understanding of God. It's like I traded in my old DNA for a new set of chromosomes."

From the corner of the ottoman, she reached her slender hand to take his, and his heart about leaped out of his chest.

Rachel said softly, "For me, the challenge is to keep walking with the good shepherd, in his way, not mine."

"With my background, it's not going to be easy."

She arranged the ice bag on his ankle with her other hand. "Why do you think so?"

"When I'm confused," said Brent, "my mind goes back to the traditions of my church; the legalistic thinking I'm familiar with. I know I'm free, but I still let myself get ensnared by it. Sometimes, I wish I hadn't started out Mormon, but I did, and it's going to affect the rest of my life."

"I guess it will, but I know God will help you every step of the way."

"My worry is . . . listen, Rachel, if you don't want to be with me, I understand. Alex says you won't even look at anyone who's not up to speed in the spiritual department."

She raised their gripped hands. "Does this look like I don't want to be with you?" He laughed, and she went on, "What Alex means is, I'm choosy about who I get involved with. I have to answer to the Holy Spirit. Believe me, God forced me out of my comfort zone when I started talking to you and Ammon in Argentina."

"He did? So, tell me, would you be put off by . . . going out with someone who's fresh out of The Church of Jesus Christ of Latter-day Saints?"

Rachel looked serious. "Your background has many good points, Brent. Don't disparage it."

"True . . . I'm self-disciplined. I listen well and I know how to blindly obey rules."

"All good virtues, if you obey God through the Holy Spirit."

"Rachel, I feel bad that I was a pompous know-it-all in Argentina. I'm embarrassed about it."

"Most of the time, I remember you were kind and considerate. Back then, I tried not to think of you as someone I'd be interested in. I had no intentions except to encourage you to find the real Jesus. But then, when you were absolutely born again and I saw what you were going through to follow Jesus, I became very interested . . ."

"So that's a yes. We're going together."

She shot Brent a bright smile, like a dart through his heart. "I'm not worried about you, Brent Young. You're growing more than many a long-time name-only Christian sitting in an ice-cold pew."

Squeezing her hand, his voice quavered when he answered. "So, I don't have to 'up my game' to go out with you?"

"With Jesus, you always have to 'up your game', but at least, we can climb those mountains together." She tilted her head, crowned in braids.

If only his foot hadn't been on the ottoman. It was too long a reach to kiss her, and he could do nothing but squeeze her hand.

Chapter Sixteen

Buon Natale

Alex noticed a solemn mood overtake Jennalee as Christmas Eve came. She excused herself to take a long walk alone in the rainy vineyard that afternoon while he stayed in the warm kitchen. Everyone needed time with God, especially when fighting disappointment. They would have to face great upheaval when they got to Utah, and he prayed they'd be ready.

Thinking of her, and their put-off marriage, he reflected what to write in his vows to her. Ideas had been milling around in his head for a while, and he tried to set them on paper. Immersed in wordsmithing, Alex looked up when he heard a knock at the back door. Through the window, he saw Jennalee, her cheeks reddened by the cold wind.

He tucked the vows inside his pocket and opened the somehow locked door. Peering at the salty tears on her cheeks, he took her tightly in his arms. "Did you walk it all out?" he asked.

She sighed. "Alex, this could've been our wedding day. I'm really sad, but I'll be okay."

Clearly, she wasn't okay. He took her hand. "C'mon, let's go up to the balcony and talk; we need all the time together we can grab before you go."

Nonna supplied the balcony with blankets to take away Rome's wintry chill and allow guests to gaze out at the grand courtyard and vineyards that spread for miles. Alex wrapped a cozy quilt around them and they stood at the railing.

"Without snow, it's not like Christmas," Jennalee said.

"Snow's rare here, Jenn, but I miss it, too."

"Back home in Utah, we deck our house in lights and put up the biggest tree we can find. Dad and Brent carry it inside and Mom and I decorate with ornaments handed down from the last three generations. This Christmas breaks new ground for me . . . but at least we're together until tomorrow."

"You sound homesick, Jenn. You must really want to get back."

"Not without you."

"When I fly back the first of January with Mom and Gabe, I'll promise to get a loan and put down deposits for the wedding. No more delays."

Jennalee looked away from him and up at the darkening sky. "You might have to, even though my parents have had a wedding fund for me since I was born. The bride pays for most of it, you know. But without my parents on board, I'm expecting trouble. Their un-blessing is the biggest hurdle yet. But I have choices in this world, and I chose you, Alex."

He hugged her tighter. "I'm happy you did," he said, his voice sober. "And I want you to know I totally respect your parents, you know I do, even though they don't like me. And why would they? A born-again Protestant is taking their daughter away from them."

He remembered Rulon Young's stern glare on prom night almost a year ago, and his nervous wife rubbing her hands.

Alex took a step back, and still wrapped in the blanket, turned to face Jennalee and hold her close. He purposely looked through her blue eyes into her soul and took her chin in his hands. "God will help us jump the hurdles in Utah. Our best plans didn't happen *here*, but he'll take care of it."

"I know," she said, "but I hate conflict and I know it's going to break out."

"We've got to believe God set up this divine appointment and will see us through, conflict or not."

She nodded. "I know. But I think we should try our best to include my family in our wedding as much as we can. That would help the whole situation."

Alex nodded. "We'll try . . . but if we've done all we can, and it's not possible . . . it's just one day in our lives, Jenn. We'll have a chance to make it up to them."

"No, you don't understand. We won't. In their eyes, not getting married in the temple can never be fixed. And we'll have to atone for it somehow."

"What have you told your parents so far?"

"I haven't even told them we're engaged, Alex. They're not in a good way right now."

"We'll tell them together when I get there. It might go better than you think." Alex tightened the blanket around them.

She shook her head slowly. "I hope so because I dread it."

"C'mon, we've got Brent and a ton of friends who'll stand by us. Pastor Ron's ready to give us pre-marital counseling and perform the ceremony. And he told me he'll talk with them."

As he looked into her eyes, a smile overtook her face.

"He did?" she asked.

"Yes. We're finally going to be together, Jenn, so let's think about *us*, no matter what happens to our wedding. What do they say about love conquering all?"

Her face brightened even further. "You're right, Alex, I can't lose hope. I love you," she said, stretching up on her toes to kiss him.

He smiled through the kiss, then said, "We'd better go downstairs. Nonna doesn't trust us alone for long, you know, especially wrapped in the same blanket. And being this close to you, I don't trust me either." He let out a sigh and opened the balcony door to usher her inside.

At that moment, a van drove up to the house, honking the horn as a bunch of young boys piled out in every direction. They waved up at them.

"It's Uncle Giuseppe, Aunt Adriana, and my cousins from Venetia. The boys must've been pent up so long in the car, they're hyper."

"I want to meet them all," she said. "And Nonna's got quite a celebration going on downstairs," she said. "It's going to be wonderful, Alex. Can you hear the clanging pots and pans?"

Alex looked at the clock in the hall. "We've got to change! We don't want to be late to our merry Christmas engagement party."

■　■　■

Jennalee was quick to put on the velvety emerald dress borrowed from Rachel. Then she bent down from her waist, twisted her thick blonde hair into a messy bun, and waltzed out into the hall. Alex closed his door and moved towards her, the ultimate handsome guy in his light-weight gray fitted Italian suit. His hair was combed but still on the wild side and five o'clock shadow covered his face. Her melancholy mood during the afternoon walk was gone, and she kissed him lightly. He took her hand to go downstairs.

As they started down, Gabe, followed by cousin Gisela, hailed them from the floor below.

"The dining room doors are barricaded and Nonna's inside," Gabe said. "She won't let anyone see the room until it's all finished."

"And Alessandro, Aunt Gina wants you in the kitchen, *pronto*," Gisela said in almost perfect English. "To choose the wine."

Jennalee followed Alex into the kitchen, trying to ignore the whispers and glances sent her way from the younger girls. It was awkward to be treated like an American movie star by his cousins, who wouldn't allow her to help in the smallest way. They didn't know how well she knew her way around a kitchen.

Uncle Lucio came up from the wine cellar with two bottles in his hands. "How many for dinner?" he asked.

"About twenty-two, I think," answered Alex. "Allow me a taste?"

His uncle uncorked a bottle and poured the light gold liquid into a wine glass. Jennalee had not yet seen Alex use his sommelier gift and watched the swirling and sniffing with curiosity. At first, Alex breathed the air above it, as though he didn't intend to take a drink. Then he lifted the glass, and sipped, showing the training Lucio had given him. Suddenly, he looked perplexed.

"Uncle . . ." he said, hesitating.

"What do you think, Alex? The best of the best from Veneto? What's wrong, my son?"

"I can't smell or taste a thing." He rubbed his nose. "Maybe a little lemon . . ."

"Nonna is cooking so much. It's the food odors; sip some water and try again."

"What food? I don't smell *anything*. Don't you see? I've lost it . . . I've lost my sense of smell." Alex's face crumpled.

"It cannot be. You are the best sommelier in Lazio," said Lucio.

Gina looked up sharply from where she stood at the sink washing lettuce. "Lucio, it's probably a temporary result of his head injury. The doctor mentioned side effects like this. He said usually the senses come back in a few months."

Lucio shook his head. "Such a loss."

Jennalee said, "It will be alright, Uncle Lucio. Alex won't need a sense of smell at college. We're going to Weber State University when we get back."

"Perhaps you are right. Still, you both must come back next year, no matter you regain your talent or no."

Alex put his hand around hers. "No worries, Uncle. Next summer, we'll be back, won't we, Jennalee?" He sounded cheerful, but his forlorn face told the truth.

Nonna swept through the kitchen, saying, "Out of the way, Lucio. They come with me." She took their hands and pulled them towards the dining room door, saying, "You must be the first to see."

Half-bowing, Nonna opened the double wooden doors with widespread arms.

As she intended, the sight took them by surprise. The high-ceilinged room had been transformed into a glittering ballroom filled with red poinsettias and tiny white lights. An enormous chandelier made the room sparkle as though each crystal had been hand-polished, and sweeping against the ceiling stood a gold-lit Christmas tree, hung with family pictures, colored glass birds and crystal angels. Each branch held lifelike snow.

The faces of the nativity scene under the tree struck Jennalee with their realism. It was the loveliest crèche she'd ever seen, with satin cloaks and gold crowns for the kings, and burlap for the shepherds.

They walked together among the tables, noting the petit fours and place cards at each chair. White roses and silver candelabra graced the red brocade-covered table centers. Music wafted down from somewhere upstairs; an orchestra playing Christmas carols.

"Oh, my word," she said, "this is magical, Alex. It makes up for everything that went wrong." Jennalee embraced Nonna, saying, "*Mille grazie. Buon Natale.*"

"At six, we expect surprise guests," Alex's grandmother said loudly.

"*Gesu Bambino*, with presents?" said one of the girls.

"Of course not," said Gisela, who was standing next to her, "Baby Jesus never brings gifts before Epiphany."

As the clock chimed six, two cars drove into the courtyard and Alex led her away from the beautiful room to the front door to meet their new guests.

Jennalee almost lost her composure when she saw a woman she recognized; the same woman who'd kissed Alex on the cheeks at the bank. Firenza. Why would Nonna invite her?

Seeing her reaction, Alex whispered, "These are family friends, Jenn, nothing more. Firenza's father has known my grandmother since childhood. In fact, rumor has it they were going together before Nonna married my grandfather."

She understood but stabs of jealousy punched her insides when she noticed Firenza's dramatic open-backed dress and the lithe figure inside it. Firenza was everything she wanted to be: confident, graceful, and sophisticated, even while wearing impossibly four-inch high heels.

Jennalee swallowed hard and thought harder. Would seeing people through the lens of jealousy possibly twist reality? Glancing at the lovely woman again, she noticed that Firenza carried herself tall, but had more than a hint of uncertainty and shyness about her.

Firenza's brother Salvatore Tarentino was quite a handsome young man; her father, balding and dignified. They greeted Alex with manly kisses. The Italian gentlemen picked up Jennalee's hand and kissed it. Firenza performed a double air kiss for them both and even whispered what sounded like a sincere 'Congratulations' directly to Jennalee.

The horrible jealousy melted. Jennalee had no reason to doubt Alex's love for her, because he loved her just the way she was. That was reality. Even if he'd been tempted to go out with the perfect Firenza, she couldn't imagine this Italian beauty in Alex's beat-up truck back in Utah.

Out of the second car poured the entire Bonadelli family. Fuglio, whose unruly mop of hair had been trimmed and slicked down, skipped into the foyer and gave Alex a long bear hug, while offering Jennalee a limp handshake.

Massimo, looking much healthier, came up and enthusiastically kissed her on both cheeks. To Alex, he said, "I must tell you, I have asked Firenza Tarentino to marry me. We are engaged, also!" He danced up on his toes as if unable to contain his joy.

This startled Jennalee so much she didn't know what to say and Alex had to speak for both of them. "Congratulations, Massimo, this is exceptionally great news. I knew your families were acquainted with each other, but I didn't know you were even going together."

At the sound of Massimo's voice, Firenza doubled back to the entrance. There she slipped her shoes off with a shy grin, leaving them neatly by the front door. Massimo held her hand, and said, "*Si*, Firenza and I met years ago. We attended many social functions together in Venezia and Roma. And only now, we decide that we are for each other."

What a gracious gesture for Firenza to even the odds by taking her heels off. Massimo was still an inch shorter than his bride-to-be, but they made a stylish couple. Jennalee felt a ready smile take over her face. "Congratulations, Massimo," she said, wholeheartedly. "And to you, Firenza."

Next, Massimo's father barreled through the front door with his petite wife. Their teen-aged daughter caught Fuglio by the ear before he tried to explore the upstairs of the mansion unaccompanied.

When Nonna rang the bell, all the guests in the house piled into the dining room, and the boys began to carry in trays of food. As they went by, Jennalee's mouth watered at the mounds of risotto and steaming pork roasts. She hadn't realized how famished she was until she smelled freshly baked bread and steaming vegetables.

Glancing at Alex, who was inhaling deeply, she noticed a heavy look of worry on his face. Was his sense of smell that important? She wished she could help him. But when he looked up into Jennalee's face and his countenance transformed into pure joy, she knew he'd be okay.

Gina came by with the cassata cake and *panettone*, setting it on a dessert table along with round Christmas *pizzella* cookies, sprinkled with powdered sugar.

Rachel went in, dressed in white, holding hands with Brent. They were such an elegant-looking couple; they seemed less shy about their budding relationship.

When the guests had been seated, Jennalee and Alex made a grand entrance at Nonna's insistence. The friend-filled room hushed for a moment then burst out with joyous voices, as the wine poured and toasts began. Spontaneous applause surged through the room, with shouts of "Bravo!" and loud whistling.

Alex stood, tapping his water glass with his knife for attention. "I have a confession to make. I didn't properly ask Jennalee Young to marry me, I only *begged* her for months."

Laughter filled the room.

"So because my proposal was less than it should be, tonight, I'd like to ask her the right way." He paused. "Jennalee, it's been a world of adventure and lovesick pain since I ran into you coming down the staircase at our high school. You've sacrificed everything - absolutely everything - to be with me, and I want you to have rich memories of this night."

Candlelight flickered in Alex's eyes. He took a white rose from the centerpiece and bowed down on his knees in front of her as the girl cousins snapped pictures with their phones. The boy cousins whooped so loud, Jennalee hardly heard Alex's words. One word from Nonna, and reverent silence filled the room.

"Jenn, will you marry me?"

The words would forever echo in her mind. Never was she at such peace about saying 'Yes' to Alex. It could have been the sip of wine, but the warmth inside her lasted the entire night. She and Alex were truly together in spirit and faith, and that, along with their lingering kiss, would have to be enough until their wedding day.

Chapter Seventeen
Arrivederci, Italia

It might have been the morning after her wedding. They could be on a Christmas honeymoon together. Instead, Jennalee looked out the rain-streaked window of the plane about to depart Fiumicino Airport without Alex. The sky was crying, too.

When they said goodbye, he whispered in her ear, "I will be there, don't lose hope. Think about good things, Jenn. Good memories, and a great future together."

In the seat next to her, Brent already snored. With no one to talk to, she willed herself to remember the joy of the night before. What was only an engagement party became a forever memory, and she was grateful to the people who'd made it so.

There was a crazy-happy moment when *Signore* Bonadelli pulled back his chair and stood up at his table, speaking slowly in English.

"I am Sergio Bonadelli. Here, my wife Amora, my son Massimo, and daughter Chiara. Alessandro, you saved my son from death. You did not choose to escape when you had a chance. You went inside his cell and carried him out of the earthquake and you saved this boy, Fuglio, too." Amora sobbed outright as her husband did a wide gesture with his hands in the air. "And all this, with a head injury."

Everyone applauded, and Fuglio, who'd been seated next to Alex, wore the widest grin of all.

Massimo's father went on. "Because of your sacrifice, my son lives, and without my son . . ." The elderly man looked down and shook his head.

More claps and cries of '*Bravo*' ensued. They raised glasses to Alex's health as Jennalee watched her hero redden and adjust his silk tie.

The big man sat down, saying, "Massimo, you have something to say."

Shorter and thinner than his massive father, Massimo took a glass of wine and looked straight at Alex.

"I was alone and dying and I heard singing. I knew God sent an angel. If I ever forget you, my friend, what is my own life worth?"

He led the crowd as they toasted Alex's bravery to cries of, '*Cin Cin*' and '*Salute*'.

Signore Bonadelli boomed when he talked. "Massimo tells me you want to be a doctor, Alessandro. To reward you for your sacrifice, I commit this day to pay for your college and medical school. From beginning to end, I pay for it. Perhaps you will go to university in Rome and become my personal physician?"

Jennalee remembered Alex's absolute surprise, and he glanced down as if he didn't deserve such a gift. Then he stood with tears in his eyes. "Sir, it's true, my dream is to be a doctor. A thousand thanks can never express how grateful I am for your gift to me. Thank you, *Signore*."

Oh, how the goosebumps covered her arms at the deafening applause! Just when it seemed to Alex that his efforts to make a living in the wine industry were over, he was rewarded for saving a life. Alex *would* become a doctor and she would be by his side.

Sunlight interrupted her thoughts, and as she adjusted the plane window's shade, she noticed they were flying above the ocean. Staring at the glittering green expanse of water, she thought about the months she'd wasted, afraid to make a decision about Alex. Because of her hesitation, he could be engaged to a different woman. Not knowing her own mind and heart might have ended their relationship forever.

In the end, though, Alex had chosen *her*, giving up his job in the family business and a near-romance with an elegant European woman. More memories assailed her tired brain.

Mm . . . the taste of the delicious cake. She'd just taken a bite of Nonna's towered *cassata*, when Massimo asked Alex, "Where do you go from here?"

Alex took her hand in a firm grip and said, "The mafia will never find me again. I'm going home to Utah to go to college with Jennalee."

Home to Utah. He'd said it, but they both knew it was more her home than his. Today, she'd land in a place where she had an historical pedigree. But Alex was in a kind of underclass there, suffering from lack of money and prestige, without the tight Utah connections she took for granted. At the thought, her eyes clouded with tears. She vowed to try harder to be his advocate in Utah, so he wouldn't feel the pain of being an outsider.

Alex would fly home in a week. Time and distance had brought them misery in the past, and she sensed they'd have a rocky homecoming with more obstacles than ever.

She noted Brent had one eye open, and jostled his elbow. "What was it like at home when you got back from your mission, Brent?"

"Well," he answered, blinking and yawning, "I hate to tell you this. . ."

"It has to do with Mom and Dad, doesn't it?"

He cleared his throat, running his fingers through his hair, which had grown longer since his mission. "Big problems."

A tightness formed in her chest. "Do you think they'll be . . . separated?" *Her* parents? This couldn't be happening.

He patted her arm. "I don't know, but it's serious. And some of it has to do with me and you not believing anymore."

"I expected them to be troubled by all of this, but not close to divorce."

He went silent for a second, then said, "They've had trouble before, Jenn, and let's pray they get through this, too. By the way, I need to tell you that I've got to leave a few days after we get home. Sorry about that, but I have to go to Price to help Ammon."

"Is he okay?"

"Not really. He's depressed, more than I've ever known him to be." Brent looked into her face. "Hey, Jenn, why are *you* sad? Alex will be home in a week."

"I know. I've been thinking about the party that should've been my wedding."

"C'mon, it was great. What I liked best was that Fuglio kid."

How the little boy's eyes had taken in the steaming food, the red glassware and twinkling Christmas lights; he'd looked like an enraptured little prince.

Brent straightened in the seat. "Wasn't it awesome that Massimo's family took him in and gave him a chance at life? Poor little kid, losing all his relatives in the quake."

She lowered her voice. "Caprice Putifaro turned out to be his aunt, and very cruel to him. You heard that she and her husband died in the aftermath of the quake, didn't you?"

"Hmm . . . I did, but didn't make the connection. You mean the woman who got Alex captured, right?"

"Yes, just like we thought, she had mafia ties, and because Alex didn't succumb to her advances, she set him up to be kidnapped." Jennalee shook her head. "But what a terrible death for any human being, to be buried in rubble." She didn't want to imagine that kind of suffering, even for people who had caused so much harm.

Brent shook his head. "Pretty bad." He looked into space. "Were you surprised by *Signore* Tarentino?"

"Totally. I couldn't believe it when he stood up and said he'd loved Nonna Luigina since they were young . . . and then proposed to her! I guess old people can get married, too, huh? And it made a double engagement party!"

"Triple. What about his daughter Firenza and Massimo, now the greatest power couple in Italy?"

"I'm truly happy for them." She peered at her brother's eyes. "I can see you miss someone, too."

He shrugged. "I'll see Rachel again when she's free. I guess you know I care about her."

"She cares about you, too; anyone can see that. I mean, the two of you were pretty close together when we walked over to see the live nativity in the village. If you hadn't had that pair of crutches, you would've been even closer. What were you talking about for so long?"

Brent took a deep breath. "Mostly about spiritual things." He paused. "Do you remember the bells, sounding at midnight? So amazing."

Everything *was* magical. She hoped with all her being that the Christmas bells, with their deep-down-into-your-soul peals of joy would foreshadow her wedding bells half a world away in Utah.

Brent yawned and tilted his head against the other side of the seat. "I've got to catch up on some sleep, so I won't be a jetlagged zombie when we get home."

Jennalee nodded, but she couldn't sleep. How hard it would be to switch from one world to another! In a few hours, they'd be home, and the old Jennalee would have to trade places with the new.

Chapter Eighteen
A Harsh Landscape

The sky was blue-black when their plane finally touched down in Salt Lake City. Brent caught sight of the capitol building and the LDS temple glowing in the cityscape. Behind them, the powdered spine of the Wasatch Front reflected the moonlight. He searched again for the temple, but it disappeared among the taller downtown buildings.

He helped Jennalee get her carry-on from the overhead rack and switched his cell phone out of airplane mode. It buzzed immediately.

"Hi, Mom. We just landed. Are you here yet?"

"Brent, I can't get there in time, so I'm sending Brother Kevin. You remember him?"

"The bishop's assistant from down the block? Yeah, that's fine. Anything wrong?"

"I'm sorry . . . I'll explain when you get here." She choked a little. "Your brothers will be happy to see you; we all will."

He sensed evasiveness and knew not to wade through repressed emotions on the phone. "Hang tight, Mom. We'll be home soon."

"She's not coming?" asked Jennalee, handing him the crutches Nonna had given him.

He shook his head.

"Dad's got to be gone somewhere." Her face pulled a frown. "They're probably getting a divorce."

"Don't say that," Brent said, a little irritated by his sister's pessimism.

"Mom will tell us more when we get home."

"I hope she tells us *everything*. She has a way of covering up for Dad and living in denial."

Brent knew it was true, but he didn't say anything. After they'd gone through customs and re-entry, they hurried past a long line of people waiting at the security checkpoint for a different concourse.

That's when Brent observed a familiar suit in the mob of people going through TSA. He limped over in that direction for a closer look and Jennalee followed with a surprised expression on her face.

The man in the suit was his father, Rulon Young, standing with his back to them.

His sister's eyes went round when she saw their father.

"Don't let him spot us," Brent whispered.

"Why not?"

"He's missing in action from our family, that's why. We'll hang back and find out where he's going."

"Do you really think we should *spy* on Dad?"

"Trust me, he won't be happy to see us anyway, not if he's up to no good."

"Oh, no, do you see? Uncle Ethan and Brother Herndon are with him."

Brent pushed her gently into a shop, where they pretended to look at Salt Lake City t-shirts as their father and the other men passed them on the other side of the corridor.

"Brother Kevin is going to wonder where we are, Brent, and our luggage is going around and around the conveyor belt downstairs."

Brent stared at her as sternly as he could. "This is important. Remember when you told me Uncle Ethan was acting strange at Grandpa and Grandma's anniversary party? I think I know why, but I want to hear it from you."

Jennalee's voice went flat. "He and Aunt Katie are having trouble because he wants another wife." Her eyes widened and she clapped her hand to her mouth. "You don't think Dad would . . ."

"No, he was always against it. But now. . . I don't know." Brent didn't know what to think. His heart sunk low in his chest as he watched their father go down an escalator.

Jennalee hid her face behind her hair. "Watch out, if he turns his head, he'll see us."

"Make sure he doesn't."

They took a calculated risk, stepping onto the escalator several steps behind their father, who was so engrossed in conversation he seemed oblivious to his surroundings. As Uncle Ethan talked to their dad, a few words wafted up the stairs. Brent caught their mom's name, 'Marjorie'.

His uncle said clearly, "Brother, you'll be blessed. She will, too, if . . ."

Brent swallowed hard. What Jennalee had revealed about their uncle's polygamous leanings scared him. It was unbelievable that he'd even have to worry about it. Surely his Dad wouldn't be tempted that way.

He had to adjust his crutches at the bottom of the escalator and stopped as Jennalee went on ahead. In a couple minutes, she doubled back and told him that the three men had settled into seats at the Las Vegas gate.

"What are you thinking?" Jennalee asked him, looking scared.

"You and I both know our religion has a peculiar history with polygamy. I pray it won't affect us, but I don't know what to think." He tried to calm his voice. "I know I'm a red-blooded American male, but it's just plain wrong. Dad's not going to get away with this. I'm going to call him on it."

"Brent, we don't know for sure. It's probably just business. But I know you've always been Mom's defender."

"I guess so. Okay, Jenn, let's go catch our ride."

■   ■   ■

"Why couldn't Mom meet us, Brother Kevin?" Brent asked his neighbor as they drove down the dark freeway.

"There's been an upset, I'm afraid," he answered, "and your father is gone on business."

"Dad's Stake President. He can't up and leave so often, can he?"

"The priesthood is in line to assist while he's gone. And relationships falter during hard times. When they do, we have to continue to believe, Brent. Your mother will tell you more."

"We saw our father at the airport," Jennalee said in a peppy voice.

115

Kevin looked surprised. "Did you speak to him?"

"No. We felt he wouldn't have wanted us to."

Kevin stared straight ahead. "I know one thing. Rebellious children cause great disappointment."

"Believe me, we know," said Brent, feeling his ears become red and hot. "But the truth is, whatever he's doing has *nothing* to do with my sister and me."

There was a long silence, until Brent split it in two. "And in case you don't remember, I got an honorable discharge from my mission, and Jennalee's getting one, too."

Kevin drove on, saying nothing until he pulled up alongside the back of their house. Brent's temper subsided, and he felt pity for this man.

"Thanks for helping my mom by picking us up this late, Brother Kevin," said Brent, as they got out. "We'll get the luggage."

"Tell Marjorie I'm praying for her, and your family."

Kevin popped the trunk. Putting his crutches aside, Brent hopped to help Jennalee lift out the luggage. Kevin waved out the window and sped away as soon as they closed the trunk.

"You'd think we had leprosy," said Brent. "Leave the bags out here. The boys can get them."

"Welcome home . . . where we no longer belong." Jennalee put her luggage down and pointed to the sidewalk. "See that?"

Brent squinted a little to see it clearer. A *For Sale* sign swung from its post in the streetlight's glare, directly in front of their house.

"Can we pray before we go inside?" asked Jennalee.

Shivering in the cold, they lifted the whole heavy mess to Jesus.

"Be strong, Jenn," said Brent, as they went inside, where their brothers in pajamas rushed forward with hugs. They asked about the crutches, but Brent downplayed the whole misadventure, even though his ankle now throbbed.

Their little brothers had grown taller, and Brent noticed they'd gone without haircuts for a long while. He'd have to take them in tomorrow for a trim.

"It's been a terrible day," Boston said in his early-teen croaky voice. He sniffed hard, in a tough, masculine way. "Mom and Dad got into a big argument. Dad knew you'd be home today, and he *still* left! Mom was so upset, she called the bishop, and he called Brother Kevin."

"Is Mom still awake?" asked Brent.

"No, she went to bed with a migraine and said she'd see you in the morning," said Logan.

Brent saw Jennalee struggling with a bag near the staircase. "You guys run and get the rest of the luggage outside and help us get it upstairs. It's time for bed. Don't worry, tomorrow will be a better day," he said.

His phone pinged as Brent locked the door and shepherded his brothers upstairs with the luggage. It was an urgent text from Ammon.

I don't know what to do. It's bad here.

Brent texted back he'd be there in a few days, but the urgency in Ammon's answer scared him.

I'm going to do something I'll regret.

Brent punched his phone number, trying to call him. No answer. He texted back.

I'll be there soon as I can. Hold on.

He knocked on the door of his sister's room, where she stood at the mirror, brushing her hair. "I have to drive to Price after I get a few hours of sleep, Jenn. Ammon sounds desperate and could be suicidal. He won't talk to me. I won't be able to see Mom, so hug her for me."

"Poor Ammon. Keep me posted," she said. "And don't worry, Brent, I can handle it here. Hey, wait a minute and I'll get you something."

He sat on her bed. She reappeared with their dad's old Velcro ankle boot and knelt to fit it on him.

"I remember," said Brent, "Dad did the same thing, only he was playing basketball." He tested the boot. "Feels great. I think I'll be fine with this, thanks for finding it, Jenn."

"Crutches, too, just in case."

"Okay. Jenn, it feels like everything's all wrong here, upside down."

"I know. Home doesn't seem like home anymore. Except for my bed. I love my bed."

"You'll sleep well then. Oh, and Jenn? Can you take the boys in for haircuts tomorrow?"

Chapter Nineteen
A Shroud on the Truth

Brent parked his car in Ammon's gravel driveway in Price and climbed the concrete stairs. At the front door, he barely touched his knuckles when it opened. There stood Ammon, wearing his long LDS underwear, with a three-day beard and scruffy hair. The neat, clean shaven companion he'd known on his mission was completely undone.

Ammon jerked his head, signaling for him to come inside. Every blind in the house was drawn, shutting out the bright morning sunshine. Brent adjusted his eyes to the darkness.

He tried not to show his dismay. "Ammon, I got four hours of sleep then I drove nonstop to get here after you texted me last night. I was afraid you'd . . . okay, tell me what's wrong."

Ammon bowed his head, his chin touching his chest. "Thanks for coming, Brent. Dad's gone. He died yesterday. Brain hemorrhage."

Grief surrounded him like a black shadow.

Back in Argentina, Brent never could have imagined what a hard road awaited Ammon. Any youthful ignorance they'd had of life's pain and suffering ended as soon as they got home. Although Brent had grown up with a fat roll of money in the bank, and Ammon with none, both of them now had overwhelming difficulties. Even a full-blown adult man should never have to deal with troubles like these.

"It's all coming down on me, Brent. First, I had to work Dad's job when he was in the hospital. If I didn't, there'd be no money to pay our bills. Now, he's dead, and I'm in the same boat." Ammon let out a huge sigh. "I wanted to finish college. I didn't want my dad's life. I hate the coal mine; you have no idea how much I hate it."

Brent heard the despair in his voice. "It'll get better, Ammon, it has to. I'll help you. You can get a scholarship; as smart as you are, you'll win a free ride."

A deep groan from Ammon showed Brent that he had gotten nowhere with his encouragement.

"You don't get it, it's impossible. I have to hold this job down. My mom can't work because of her weak heart. And would you believe, she's already picked out a wife for me."

"She can't do that, Ammon."

"Brent, if I get married, there will be kids, and I'll be stuck here forever. Sometimes I wish I could end it all."

"Don't talk like that. You're one of the best guys I know and you'll make it through this. Right now, you need sleep." Brent put his arm around him. "I'm sorry about your dad, Ammon. The doctors thought he'd make it, didn't they?"

Ammon slowly nodded. "They were going to let him out of the hospital today. He was supposed to go back to his job in a few months, but the head injury did more damage than they'd thought."

"How's your mom?"

"Holding up. My sisters went with her to talk to the funeral director. I was asleep when he . . . when it happened. I just got off graveyard shift. They woke me up to tell me, and I haven't slept since."

Ammon's already burdened soul could hardly come up for air.

"Okay, I'm sticking with you through this," said Brent. "And that means I'm calling the shots the way I see them. Need a pill to sleep? We'll get your doctor to give you something."

"No, thanks, Brent. With you here, I already feel better. I'll sleep once I hit the pillow. You don't know how much you help me. Thanks."

"Good. When one of us is down, the other picks up the burden. We're used to watching each other's backs, aren't we?"

"Are we ever? I'll owe you big time after this. Hey, I almost forgot to tell you a new development. This janitor at the mine, Mike; he thinks he saw something the night Dad was hurt. I don't know if anyone will believe him, but it's worth a try."

Ammon swept his hair back, and his face reappeared.

"What did he see?"

"He was cleaning on the night shift when he thought he saw three men push Dad onto the coal car tracks. The trouble is, he'd just come around the corner and it happened so fast that his memory's kind of sketchy."

"Wow, this is big. Does he know who the men were?"

Ammon wrote two names on a piece of paper and handed it to Brent. His expression turned grim. "This is in case something happens to me or Mike. He doesn't know the third guy, and *he* was more or less the leader."

"Two names! That's great. Hey, nothing is going to happen to you, not on my watch. And Mike's an official witness. I need to talk to him and put you both under protection. I'll take you out of here to keep you safe."

Ammon raised his brows. "Sounds good, because I think they're going to come after me. I have no friends at the mine; the place is spooky. Mike's the only one who would even speak to me."

"I believe it. From now on, this is a murder case, got that? And the perps know it, too. Serious business. Where does your witness live?"

Ammon led Brent towards the kitchen window. "See the blue house? That's Mike Vargas's."

"Get dressed," said Brent. "We're going to talk to him."

■　　■　　■

A week later, on a cold January morning, Brent put on a suit for the first time since his mission. Attending Otto's quick graveside service was the least he could do for his friend. Afterwards, he planned to drive Ammon and Mike to Salt Lake City for their safety.

Staring at the cold ground during the service, it surprised him how intensely he missed Rachel, far away in Italy. If only she were with him. Texting and Facetime weren't enough, even every day.

What would Rachel think of Utah's close-knit LDS communities? Would she notice that at Otto Carr's memorial, where you'd think you'd see true grief, there were no tears for the dead man other than from the family? Feelings ran cool when the deceased man was judged to be a drunken gambler. The whole thing made him sad, both at Otto's death and because his life had seemingly been without meaning.

Ammon looked like he'd stepped out of a Dickens novel with his hair slicked back from his gaunt face. His dark suit's lapels were streaked with salt from the tears on his cheeks, blown there by the freezing wind. This had to be agony for Ammon; his whole life had been cruelly examined, living in the fishbowl that was Price.

Anyone who saw Otto's disheveled wife could tell he'd been a bad husband. Her stoic daughters shifted their feet in the cold, wearing long skirts, holding their eyes to the ground. Their father would be buried on this desolate hill and only his family would miss him. Even *they* would be less sad in a few months, relieved of the complications he'd brought them. His legacy was grinding poverty.

Brent looked at each of the attendees' faces. If any of the perpetrators of Otto's so-called accident were there, he may be able to spot them. He daydreamed about winning the case to bring Ammon's family out of their slump, but the eulogy interrupted his thoughts.

"Heavenly Father," a young bishop prayed in a grave King James voice, "with the authority vested in me as a Melchizedek priesthood holder, I dedicate and consecrate this ground as holy and protected until the resurrection of the dead. . ."

This sounded like the sleepy formal prayer he'd heard all his life, and it troubled him. *Melchizedek* . . . he'd read something in the New Testament about this high priest in ancient times. Was the Mormon idea of him correct?

The bishop went on. "May the Lord comfort this family and direct them to follow their covenants and ordinances as taught by the Prophet Joseph Smith. Then and only then will they be united with their husband and father in a forever family. I speak this in the name of Jesus Christ."

Deep down, Brent's spirit disagreed. *Jesus is the only One who saves, not the ordinances of man.* A year ago, when the gospel of John came alive to him with fiery truth, it freed him from trying to be good. The rest of the New Testament clinched the deal. And the LDS Melchizedek priesthood was unnecessary. He'd underlined it in his new Bible. Jesus alone is our High Priest, there is no need for any other. He sighed. No one here wanted to understand any of these things.

As crystals of dirty snow swirled around them, Ammon's family shook hands with the somber congregants. The look on the bishop's face showed he was relieved the service had ended.

Out of nowhere, a young woman strolled up to the gravesite carrying an enormous flower wreath, outshining any of the smaller arrangements. Brent had to admit she surpassed any of the women attendees, too.

She wore a white wool coat and red beret, and dark curls wisped around her hat. Bending in a graceful way, she placed the wreath near Otto Carr's grave.

He saw Ammon look sharp and offer his hand to her. They spoke a few minutes, their faces close together in the whipping wind. Then, arm in arm, they walked back to her car where Ammon opened the door for her.

Brent waited a few seconds, then sprinted over to where Ammon gazed with a sad smile at the departing car.

"Tell me who she is," he said, his breath coming out in freezing puffs.

"Sophie Voskopoulos. I've known her since fifth grade."

"The Greek Orthodox girl you told me about? You never mentioned how gorgeous she is."

A wee smile appeared on the otherwise stricken face. "Brent, you know she's off limits. I mean, she's the oldest daughter of the best baker in town, Dmitri Voskopoulos. You can't get more Greek than that . . . and less LDS."

"Well, even so, it was awesome of her to bring that wreath."

Ammon nodded and shrugged at the same time. "She works in the flower shop downtown and heard about Dad because she arranged most of the flowers for the funeral. I always liked Sophie . . . you know, as a friend."

As Ammon stared wistfully in the direction Sophie had gone, Brent could see he more than liked her. Putting on the pressure, he said, "You know her pretty well?"

"Yeah, we lived next door in fifth and sixth grade. We lost track of each other when she moved across town, but those two years, we did everything together. We ended up at Carbon High School together, but hardly saw each other. Couldn't, you know."

"Why don't you ask her out?"

Ammon's brows went up in a question mark. "Brent, you know I can't. She knows it, too. When we were kids, it didn't matter; we used to sit outside on the porch and talk about our dreams, sometimes for hours." His mouth formed a grim line. "None of it matters anymore."

"Not true, Ammon, it *does* matter. You can't give up your dreams."

Ammon looked up, where large cumulus clouds moved across the sky. "We had a lot in common. Number one, we both wanted to leave Price for a better life. We used to read the same books on purpose so we could talk about them. And art. Sophie explained Renaissance paintings to me, and icons and why she likes Impressionism."

"She sounds like pure gold, compared to a lot of girls. Listen, I think you should take her out for a movie and ice cream . . . as a friend. You need someone who knows you in a deep way right now. You shouldn't let her get away."

Ammon pursed his lips like he was chewing on the suggestion. "When I knew her, life was simple. I don't think she'd want to go out with me now, not since I'm . . . a college dropout with no future except working in a coal mine. I'll never get out of Price."

"Listen, she wouldn't have come here if she didn't care about you. Tell her about Argentina, our soccer boys, our adventures in the slums. You have stories to share, years of catching up."

"Maybe."

"She knew your dad?"

Ammon's eyes looked up in memory. "Dad always liked her. Mom, too."

"Look, all this religious stuff is complicated," Brent said, "but I think . . . no, I know . . . she's worth the risk."

"You're saying there's nothing to the problem that I'm LDS and she's Greek Orthodox?" Ammon's face reddened.

"I used to think it was an insurmountable problem," said Brent, "one that no bridge could ever cross. But now I think different. What if God himself brought her here today? Maybe he's bigger than our religions put together. In fact, I know he is."

Ammon's Argentina smile came back full and strong, a trace of hope in his eyes.

Chapter Twenty
Never Afraid

"More of the same with your family, isn't it? Doubting and more doubting."
Bishop Crosby stopped pacing around his plush office to glare at Jennalee and
her mother sitting stiff-backed on the couch. The bishop's wife, looking stern,
sat across from them in a chair. She had long since lost her church smile,
making Jennalee feel alone, walking on permafrost.

It had definitely not been the homecoming of her dreams. She'd wanted
to tell the world about the joy of her engagement, but couldn't. She put her
palm on Alex's ring, now back on its chain. Though it would have to be
hidden until the time was right, it comforted her.

Utah had always been friendly and welcoming, but today Jennalee became
aware she was no longer inside the fold, but on the outside. It was a scary
thought because it changed everything she'd known, and she prayed for
courage.

Jennalee hated seeing her mother have to sit through this hearing with her
once-perfect daughter, now considered an unbelieving doubter. The bishop's
accusatory tone must've gone straight to her mother's heart because her head
hung downward in shame. She wished her mom could feel the supernatural
peace she felt.

She knew that the bishop's judgement of her was completely wrong. All
she could think of was freeing herself from the glaring eyes of the bishop and
his wife's disapproving frown. But first, she had to stand and face the

accusations against her, the way she'd told Alex she would.

Straightening her shoulders and raising her head high, she stood up. The man glowered at her and she met his gaze, unflinching.

"Jennalee Young, in your own words, tell us why you left your mission after one month. According to witnesses, you ran away."

She willed herself to be brave and words formed inside her mind. "It's simple, Bishop Crosby. I had to rescue someone. I could see no other choice at the moment."

"Why didn't you take time to talk to your mission president?"

"I couldn't . . . there was no time."

The man's mouth formed a twisted scowl. He tried to stare her down, then said, "Your mother says you came home to help the family. We understand she needs your aid since your father's often away on business. Is this true?"

Jennalee gave her mother a quick glance. "It's true, but as I said before, I take full responsibility for running away. I only found out later how much my mother needed me. My father . . ."

"Yes, your father, Stake President Young, has added a statement to your file."

Even though Dad was out of town, he'd had to say something about her behavior. She was sure Bishop Crosby's attitude was affected whatever his President had said.

The bishop's thin lips formed a line. "Sister Young, your reasoning does not excuse your disobedient behavior. However, attitudes aside, I find there was legitimate justification for you to leave your mission. Family first, family forever."

"Bishop Crosby, if you knew you had to leave a commitment to save the life of someone you cared about, you'd have chosen to quit like I did."

His steely eyes practically closed shut. "I choose to accept your mother's reason for your behavior. You'll be excused and . . . honorably discharged. Miss Young, there is no need to report on your mission before the ward during Sacrament meeting on Sunday. I'll get the word out about . . . your honorable discharge."

Next to her, she heard her mother's breath release and her own heavy dread lifted.

"Thank you, Bishop. My reasons are complex, but I'm grateful to be discharged in a good way."

The man glanced at his wife, whose church smile returned.

"Jennalee," she said, sweeter than maple syrup, "since your mother and I are close friends, I think it's best you remain silent about any other reasons you left your mission, complex or not. We know about you here."

Under pressure, Jennalee agreed. How she wished she could tell the marvel of how Jesus had transformed her life and made her free! *When you are raised up and born-again, you know it!* But sitting in the office of the LDS bishop, it was obvious her story straight out of the third chapter of John would have to wait. The all-knowing God would give her a chance to speak out, and soon, she'd wear her engagement ring with pride.

■　　■　　■

The day finally arrived when Alex would land in Utah. She wished he'd been here all this time to help her shoulder the deep heaviness after meeting with the bishop. Forced to play a role at home, and act like nothing had changed, she felt like bursting the seams to be her real self. But Mom couldn't handle her news, not with being an emotional wreck. Jennalee would have to be sweet and dependable. She didn't want to upset her any more than she already was.

That morning as she fixed the boys' breakfast, she keenly felt the burden of her mom's depression and migraines which confined her to her bed. Dad and Brent had been gone the entire week, leaving her alone with the responsibility of her brothers. Her family, the former foundation of her life, was ready to fall apart, but she'd have to remain strong.

She glanced at the clock. Alex would arrive at the airport in a couple of hours, and she may have to text him that she couldn't be there. Having no time to spend alone with Jesus, she could barely lift a prayer. She'd ask him to pray.

Later, she'd talk to Alex, and once he understood how bad things were, she hoped he'd agree to delay their plans till her mom was better, and her dad came home. They couldn't have a wedding in the middle of these chaotic family problems. It was impossible.

During breakfast, her brothers bickered with each other, and she had to correct them several times. Making sure they had their lunches and winter gloves, she got them off to school for the first day after winter break.

An hour afterwards, as Jennalee wiped the table, her mother appeared in the kitchen, wearing her bathrobe and slippers. It was hard to watch such an organized, pretty woman become more disoriented with each day.

"Mom, are you feeling better? I got the boys off to school, and then I want to go to the airport to meet Alex. I can stay here if you need me, but . . ."

"Tell him you can't come," said her mother. "I need you here, Jennalee. I didn't get much sleep. Who can sleep with these troubles?"

"Troubles?"

"First, there's you. I'm not as naïve as you think, Jennalee. You've been thousands of miles away, alone with this Alex, and I know you've slept with him. I can accept this, Jennalee, but . . ."

Her face burned. "No, Mom. Listen to me! I have not done anything wrong."

Jennalee looked directly into her eyes.

"Mom, you have to believe me. Alex doesn't force physical stuff like every other guy I know. And if you want to know the truth, I'm in love with him for many reasons, but a major one is because he has self-control and wants to wait. It's been hard, Mom, but we're pure, we're choosing the right, and . . ."

Her mom turned away and plopped herself into a chair at the table. Jennalee sighed and went to the refrigerator.

"Then, of course, there's Brent," said her mom. "The whole ward knows about his apostasy because he stood up at Sacrament meeting and said it. What a terrible time in our family! Our two oldest children, straying from the true Gospel. What did I do wrong?"

Jennalee set a glass of orange juice in front of her mom, but she pushed it away.

"Please come to Sacrament meeting with your family, Jennalee," said her mother. "The bishop said you won't have to talk about your failed mission."

"I'll think about it, Mom."

"If you don't come back, your father is sending you to live with Grandma in Lehi. You can't go, because I need you here."

The awful ultimatum of being sent away was simply her parents' plans to keep her away from Alex, and she knew it.

Her voice shook. "Mom, I respect your wishes and . . . of course I'll go to Sacrament meeting with you this Sunday."

Her mom looked past her, grimacing in pain. She clutched her middle with her arms.

"Are you okay, Mom?"

"It's the same old pain. Nothing, really," her mom said. "It's going away, but it'll be back." She sighed heavily.

The doorbell rang and her mother slapped her hand to her mouth. "It's Opal Taylor," she said. "I forgot she wanted to come over today to discuss . . . Relief Society business."

Jennalee left her mother in the kitchen and went to open the front door.

"Welcome home, Jennalee," Opal said in her quiet authoritative way. Opal, a few years older than her mother, had raised six kids, including a disabled daughter.

"Thanks. Mom's in the kitchen. Go on in, she'll be happy to see you."

Opal strode forward, as Jennalee hung back, resolving to listen as she put away Christmas ornaments from the dried tree in the adjacent living room.

"I forgot you were coming, Opal," Mom said. "Sorry I'm in my bathrobe."

"I had to come and tell you, Marjorie," said the neighbor. "Our suspicions have been verified."

Their voices went low, but a moment later, Jennalee heard hysterical weeping and realized it was her mother. The wailings from her mother, who, in ordinary circumstances never shed a tear, echoed in her ears. She rushed back into the kitchen. Her mother's head was in her hands, as Opal stood beside her.

"I need to go, I left Tina by herself," Opal said, in a strangely business-like tone. "I'll be back after my husband gets home. Marjorie . . . Jennalee's here for you."

She started to leave and Jennalee followed her.

"Please wait," said Jennalee. "What happened? This is way more than Relief Society business."

When Opal circled around, her eyes darkened. "What do you want to know, Jennalee?" she asked sharply.

"Is this something about my dad?"

"Yes. If you must know, he's been seen with a brassy young blonde in Las Vegas. That's all we know so far."

"We? Who exactly knows?"

"I have a sister in Vegas, whose husband is an undercover officer. He took this as a side job. Your mother needed to know the facts."

How she wanted to tell this woman that her loyal dad would never do such a thing, but after seeing him in the airport, there had been little doubt he was up to something.

Opal began a speech she'd probably held in for a while. "Jennalee, it doesn't help you're dating a non-Mormon and left your mission for him. The rumor mill says it all. You don't know what stress and worry you and your brother are causing."

Jennalee felt her neck heat up. "Wait a minute . . ."

"You must regain your sacred covenants, Jennalee. That's the real reason why your family's having problems."

This statement went into Jennalee like a dart, and she wobbled like *San Sebastiano,* the martyr killed with arrows.

"Miss Opal," she managed to say. "My parents' problems have nothing to do with my temple covenants."

"Dear, we all know weak faith causes bad things to happen. And how can you even think of living without your mother and father in eternity?"

Jennalee held up her hand at the barrage of words. "Please listen. I fell in love with a non-Mormon and I love Alex more than anyone on earth."

"More than the family God gave you? The one you *chose* in your pre-terrestrial life? You must always follow the Prophet, Jennalee. *Always,* even when it's not in your best interest. Once you start doubting the prophets you will fall into sin and fail in all you do."

"Miss Opal, in Italy, I discovered how to live life in a new way."

"Honey," Opal said in a sweeter tone, "I understand it was the first time you were away from home. Anyone is impressionable and under temptation when far away. But, I must warn you; you're stumbling into grave error, worse than your father's, and you're bringing *disgrace* on your family. I believe I speak for your mother on this."

Jennalee felt more hot spots on her neck. "I don't see it that way at all. If anything, I'm bringing *grace* to this family. And we don't know for sure whether Dad is committing adultery. I know I'm not."

Opal shot her a suspicious look. "I hope you're not lying, Jennalee. Of course, you know full well your father isn't perfect. Even the Prophets aren't. Some have an imprecise understanding of God's universe but we must always follow them anyway, *unquestioning*."

Jennalee gulped for air. "I've learned to base my life on the written Word of God. It's translated absolutely correctly except you have to have eyes to see it and ears to hear it. And when the time's right, I *will* marry the man I love."

"The time will never be right, Jennalee. Not for time, and not for eternity. God's plan for your spiritual progression is not the path you're on. My advice to you would be to flee away from these evangelical Protestants who have no knowledge of the true Gospel." The woman looked at her with such enormous disapproval, Jennalee felt a sob rise in her throat, though somehow, she held her ground.

"You're not hearing me, Miss Opal. I *am* following God's true plan for my life."

"You're not. It can't be, because without a temple wedding you'll never be able to join your family in Celestial heaven. You'll be in a lesser place or even outer darkness with a persecutor of the Restored Gospel, the one true religion. Do you want that?"

"Just because Alex helped me compare my religion to what the Bible says does not mean he's a persecutor of LDS people. He loves Mormons. And I don't care about not getting married in the temple."

Opal's mouth opened in shock. Jennalee took the moment to close the conversation. "I've got to get back to Mom, and you've got to get back to Tina. Goodbye."

Everything about her return home had gone haywire, the opposite of her experience in Italy. She felt crushed, but she would never allow this to take away her love for the true biblical Jesus.

Jesus, be as alive to me now as you were in Italy.

■　　■　　■

Minutes later, Jennalee sat at the table across from her mother. Back in high school, she used to ignore anything wrong at home, yet hard facts now stared her down. She'd never seen her mother so sad and vulnerable.

Her mom's voice choked in sobs. "For a long time, I suspected Rulon was unfaithful. I asked for proof and Opal handed it to me."

The photo in front of her was Dad alright, and in it, he walked close to a voluptuous blonde. The sorrow of their words and the damaging photo hung awkwardly in the air between her and her mother, causing neither to say anything for a minute.

"And to think I had six children with him. . ." She let out a wail. "And only *he* knows my name."

Jennalee assumed her mom meant her temple name, the secret one that only her husband had been entrusted with during their marriage sealing in the temple. With this name, he would call her to rise up to be his wife in Celestial heaven . . . if he chose to.

"Did you ask Dad for an explanation?"

"No, how will he be able to explain this picture?" Her mother wiped her eyes with a tissue.

"He may have a good explanation, Mom. You should give him a chance."

Her mom shook her head. "Did the boys tell you how much your father and I fought over money the last few months? He's taken it all. Your savings, Brent's, and all of the boy's college money. There's nothing left."

Jennalee's heart recoiled. "Wait, Mom . . . my wedding fund, too?"

Her mother's mouth formed an angry line. "He's spent it on another woman when he told me it was for a new business."

Jennalee's heart beat wildly. "Listen, Mom, the one thing I'm here for is to help you and the boys. I can put my life on hold for a while. But I will not forget Alex and our plans together, money or not."

Her mother looked at her blankly.

Jennalee took a deep breath. "Even if you don't understand how much I've changed, I love you, Mom. Will you give Alex a chance?"

"I'll try . . . ," her mother started to say, when pain overtook her face. She doubled over, groaning and clutching her stomach.

"What can I do for you, Mom?"

Her mother huffed out air and said, "It's the worst it's ever been."

"Okay, this time I'm taking you into Urgent Care," said Jennalee. "We'll be back by the time the boys get home from school." With a lump in her throat, she realized seeing Alex today would be impossible.

Chapter Twenty-One
Heavy Trials

During the week between Jennalee's flight and Alex's, she'd called and texted him often in the beginning, with *'good to be home'* messages. Then came apologies about being busy. Towards the end of the week, her texts and calls were shorter and far between. Alex tried to call at good times for Mountain Standard Time, but even when she answered, she only had a couple minutes to talk, because her brothers needed her. They weren't babies . . . why was she too busy to talk?

He noticed the Great Salt Lake appear as the plane neared the airport. Chafing with annoyance, he looked at his mother next to him, just rousing herself from a nap.

The same grim fears he'd had before ensnared his mind. In the forefront was the nagging worry about Jennalee being vortexed back into her family's religion. If her faith and knowledge of the biblical Jesus had just gone skin-deep, she'd waver, even with her supernatural experience. The strange twisting of mixed-in truth coming from man's religion might be too deceptive for a new believer to sort out under duress.

He slumped in seat 14A. Why did he think their engagement would be enough to clinch the marriage? If only they'd married in Italy and come home together.

As they descended, the gray sky resembled the color of a bruise and melancholy flooded into him. His Mediterranean blood hated bleak winters, but even if he resisted, Utah was again his home. He should be happy since this was the very place where he'd pursued his love until he'd won her, in spite of the culture and harsh circumstances.

His mother woke and said to him, "What's wrong? You don't look glad to be home."

"Something's up with Jenn."

"Oh? I imagine she's trying to adjust to life in Utah. And you're starting college together, which can be stressful. But the Bonadellis' gift of tuition is a miracle, son. You're excited, aren't you?"

"I am, but it's hard to concentrate without Jennalee making plans with me." Should he tell her his fears?

"Mom?" he inquired, intending to follow with what really bothered him. The sound of the landing gear coming down interrupted him. He doubled back. Wasn't he an adult who didn't need his mom's help? Instead he said, "Can you pray for me and Jenn? I have a bad feeling now that we're back in Utah."

She peered at him above her red reading glasses. "What are you worried about, Alex?"

"For one, making a living. Jennalee will be my wife, and I need to take care of her *pronto*. I'll get my Starbucks job back until something better comes up, but it's not much."

"Alex, you two can squeeze by like your dad and I did. You can have a small wedding, like the one that didn't happen."

"Maybe you're right. I'm unsure at this point. She's busy with her family and it's been hard to talk. Anyway, I can hardly wait to get off this plane and see her."

"You two will be married somehow," his mom said as the plane touched the runway.

As soon as he took his phone out of airplane mode, it buzzed. Jennalee texted she couldn't come to the airport. Disappointment piled on top of his other worries.

"Jennalee can't meet me, her mom's sick. I'll have to go with you. Who's going to pick us up? I hope it's not Carl." Alex was aware his mom had broken up with Carl, but hoped the annoying man wouldn't make a reappearance.

"Where have you been? I've had no contact with Carl for a long time, Alex. I had to learn that not everyone who calls themselves Christian can be trusted." His mom smiled brightly. "No, no. A new *trustworthy* friend dropped us off and is picking us up. You remember Jeff Allred?"

Alex nodded. "Yes, I do." Jeff was almost like his dad; kind, wise, fun to be with.

"You're a little surprised," said his mom. "I should've told you that we've been going out all summer while you were in Italy. And it all started at your graduation party."

"I guess I *was* in my own little world over in Italy. Wow, Mom."

"Jeff's twins come over every other Sunday for brunch. Gabe loves them; you will, too."

"Sounds like you're getting serious."

She visibly relaxed her shoulders. "'Serious' is such a harsh word for something so wonderful, don't you think? There's got to be a better word for caring for each other."

"There is, Mom, but I don't think you're ready to say it yet."

■　■　■

Whether it was his own need or pressure from his mom, Alex sat in front with Jeff on the way home, and his worries spilled out. Jeff would get it, having once been a Latter-day Saint himself.

"The question at hand is what's going on in Jennalee's mind," Alex said. "I mean, what if she goes back to being LDS? I don't understand why she would after her experience with Jesus, but there's a strong pull . . ."

"It may be that she's just caught in a repeating pattern I see in my practice as a counselor," Jeff said. "It happens more often in strict religions. Families can become enmeshed with each other and the kids have a hard time leaving. Sometimes parents control their kids long after they're adults. It happened to me and my ex."

"You think that's what's happening? Because I feel like she's shutting me out. Again."

"I'm just saying over-parenting can cause a lot of issues."

"Well, Gabe and I weren't over-parented, we practically raised ourselves," Alex said, looking back at his mom.

"I heard you, young man," she said from the back seat, "and you know my method was to go to the Lord about everything."

Jeff directed his voice to the rear view mirror. "And because of you, Gina, they're both great young men."

His mom beamed.

"Thanks, Jeff," said Alex. "But I wish we had already gotten married, because her parents would have to accept us, wouldn't they?"

Jeff Allred looked at him sideways. "No, they might never accept you. You and Jennalee should brace yourselves for that reality. Your best move would be to love them unconditionally and include them in everything you can, Alex. And try to think about them more positively. They love their daughter and thought they'd passed on their religious values to her. Since she totally changed after she met you, you can see why they're disturbed, right?"

"Yes . . . I guess Mom would be mad if I'd done the same thing."

"And you know how important weddings are to LDS families. It's a good thing you didn't get married first because they would've felt completely left out. It won't be easy to get, but you two need some form of blessing from her side."

"How are we supposed to get it?"

"Think of it this way: you have a long future with a wife you love. Fifty years or more! And she loves her family. You need their approval, even if it's lukewarm."

"It's not going to happen. So far, they don't like me, and it's hard for me to like them."

"They don't *know* you, Alex. And you don't know them. God has this in his hand. He'll show you an opportunity to bring them around."

An opportunity? All he could see ahead was strife.

Jeff briefly turned to look at him for a second. "Have you ever thought of life with God as a deep flowing river? You have to float along with the current, not against it, because if you do, you'll be thrown around on the rocks or get yourself stuck." He paused. "Alex, God knows the river. He knows exactly where it's going and intercedes whenever you allow him to. Prayer and obedience result in God's power in your life. He doesn't just throw you a little help from time to time, he's in the water with you, every day, every moment, and every breath."

"Are you telling me to go with the flow?"

Jeff smiled. "His flow, not yours."

■　■　■

Jennalee cried so hard over the phone Alex couldn't understand her. He held his cell closer and sat down on the old couch in their Kaysville living room. He'd never known her to sound so panicked.

"Jenn, it's okay, I got your text. We can see each other later. Heck, I've got jet lag anyway." He hoped his tone would calm her.

"I'm at Urgent Care with Mom right now. And there's more trouble. I'll tell you later because she's coming out of X-ray now. Sorry, Alex, I've got to go. Bye."

After the quick dramatic call, Alex wandered outside and sat on the cold concrete cube of a porch to think. His 1950's rented house was entirely unlike his family villa outside Rome. Would he always feel like a stranger in Utah? And how much would this trouble of Jennalee's change their plans?

He texted her: *I'm here for you. Tell me what's wrong. I love you.*

She called him back.

"They took her in a wheelchair to the lab. I think I have a few minutes." She paused. "Alex, it looks like I can't go to college with you. Not this semester. And we can't get married, not yet."

It felt like she'd punched him in the gut. "Why not?"

"My parents are in such a bad way that we have to wait. And college for me right now. . . I can't go."

"Do you want me to come over tomorrow and tell them we're engaged, like we planned?"

"No, they're not ready. Dad isn't even in town. I was brave in Italy, but I'm losing courage here, Alex."

He felt his voice go tight. "I thought we'd worked through this, even though I sensed you might get enmeshed again with your family." He hadn't meant to say it quite that way. "I mean . . ."

"What do you mean, *enmeshed?*" Her voice became a bit shrill. "Mom's sick, and Dad's away on business. I have to take care of my brothers because Brent went to Price to help a friend. I'm the only one who can be here and do this, Alex."

"I know, Jenn. I'm sorry for my choice of words; I'm just disappointed. Can't we keep the wedding in May? On your grandfather's birthday?"

"I wish we could. This is really complicated and I can't explain it on the phone. We have to postpone our wedding. Alex, I thought you'd understand. It's not about us right now."

Hot anger climbed up his neck to his ears. "Jenn, what if we'd been married in Italy? Then, I'd be with you, helping like they were my own family."

She paused. "My family's breaking up and it's a chaotic mess here. It's best if you register for college without me, Alex."

"What about *us?* Are *we* breaking up? After all we've been through? Is it something I said?" It must be. She wouldn't break up with him unless he'd done something wrong.

Her voice quivered. "Alex, it's nothing you did or said. Never think that."

"Why are you shutting me out?" Hurt began to gnaw him from the inside.

"It's my problem . . . not yours. You can't solve it. I've got to call Brent about Mom. I'll talk to you later. I don't see how we can get married now. There's no way."

"Listen to me, Jenn, it's four months away. We can make it a small wedding, can't we?"

There was no answer.

"Well . . . I hope your Mom is okay," he said. "I'll be praying, Jenn. About everything." His phone went back to his home screen as soon as he said it.

What could be so bad at home she'd compromise their future together? In a week, it felt like she was no longer his. He would have to strip away her faulty reasoning and find out why she'd put him on the outside again. If only she'd realize that his love for her went deeper than any fear.

Chapter Twenty-Two
Treading Water

Brent noticed Ammon's bedazzlement inside the opulent lobby of the office building of Young, Taylor, and Merrill in downtown Salt Lake. The way he stopped in his tracks and stared at the ornate marble walls and floors, Ammon seemed like he was under a spell. The witness, Mike, took a selfie in front of the fountain splashing in the glass-ceilinged atrium where living palm trees reached for the sun.

"Don't share that on social media, Mike, or they'll know where you are," said Brent, trying not to sound nervous. "You guys wait here while I go up to talk to my cousin Moab and find out about the deposition. Be right back."

As he waited for one of four elevators, his phone rang. It was his sister. "Slow down, I can't understand you." He ditched the elevator area and went into the stairwell for privacy.

"Brent?" she said, so loud it hurt his ear. "You've got to come home and help. I'm still in Urgent Care with Mom and the boys are alone at home watching TV."

"The boys are fine with Boston, he's fourteen now. And I'll be home in a few days when I make sure Ammon and Mike are safe. I'm on my way right now to Moab's office. We're probably filing the case tomorrow morning."

"Sounds serious, but you're needed here, too."

"Jenn, this case morphed into first-degree murder. You can manage a few more days, can't you? You said you could."

She sighed. "I guess I'll have to. How's your ankle?"

"Better, the walking boot's good. Hey, I've got to get back anyway because there's a problem with my bank. For some reason I can't use my debit card because of low funds. Doesn't make sense. I had to charge gas and a hotel room on my credit card."

"Brent, I hate to tell you this, but Dad took our money for his new business."

"*Our* money? Yours and mine?"

"And the little boys', too. All the money Grandpa Young saved for us is gone. There's nothing left for college. And nothing for my wedding."

He couldn't believe his father would do this. Drawing a breath, he said, "I'll ask Moab for a job. He offered me one before."

"Well . . . I wanted to start college next week with Alex and now I have no money. And our wedding's off . . . for who knows how long?"

"Dad will have to answer for this."

"I have to stay here and take care of the kids. And Mom's got severe abdominal pain. They're doing tests."

"Let me know the results."

"Okay, I will. Also Brent, there's proof about Dad. There's a picture of him with a blonde woman."

Brent sighed into the phone. "I'm not surprised. I'll get home as fast as I can. Have you told Alex? He can help while I'm gone."

She didn't answer.

"Jenn? You didn't tell him about any of this, did you? I suggest you stop protecting Dad and the perfect image of our family. Alex needs to know the truth."

"I'm not protecting Dad. It's just that some people have said hurtful things, and I don't think Alex needs to be involved."

"You didn't break up with him, did you?"

"Brent, we can't get married with this going on. He doesn't understand and says I'm enmeshed with my family."

"We *are* enmeshed, Jennalee. Our parents' marriage crisis isn't ours. We both know their problems have been going on for years. Now's the time for you to be with Alex."

"This is *family*, Brent. How can I not help them?"

He gave in. "I know. Realistically, we have to help, within limits."

"What kind of limits?"

"Jenn, you found the right guy. Don't give him up for anything. God is in this; Alex can help you, no matter what Mom or anyone else says."

A long silence followed before Jennalee responded. "Okay. You're right."

"And Alex is ready to take the flak from anybody, including Dad. He's used to it. Don't try to protect him. Make sure you call the poor guy fast and straighten it out."

"Brent, I don't want anyone to hurt him, but you're right, I need him with me. Don't worry, I'll call him as soon as we get home. Hey, have to go. Mom's being wheeled out to the car. Thanks, Brent . . . for everything."

Brent had no more entered the hallway to Moab's office when his phone rang again. Alex. He picked up. Sure enough, the poor guy was panicked about Jennalee.

"I just got off the phone with her," Brent told him. "She told me she'll call you when she gets home in a little while to clear things up."

"You mean she didn't break up with me? I don't get it."

"There's a lot going on with our family, and I told her you'd rather share the burden with her than be without her. That's right, isn't it?"

"Absolutely," said Alex, "I'm all in, bad times or good."

"I bet she didn't tell you her wedding money's gone. My dad took it with him to Vegas, along with every cent of Grandpa Young's college savings for his grandkids."

Alex whistled. "She didn't tell me. Hmm . . . makes sense now."

"Sorry our family's in a mess, but I know she'll stick by you in the end."

"I just want her back."

"I know. She'll call you in about thirty minutes. Hey, I've got an appointment. Hate to cut you short."

"It's okay. *Ciao*."

■　　■　　■

In the men's seventh floor restroom, Brent splashed his face with water, sweeping back his thick brown hair with his hand. Seeing himself in the mirror, he hoped his tieless shirt and suit coat would not seem underdressed in the luxurious office.

His uncle's receptionist wore red lipstick and a navy-blue suit, leaving him with the impression that he was in a city as cosmopolitan as New York. She pressed a key on her computer to summon his cousin, who burst through a door within a few seconds.

"You're back," said Moab, yanking his hand and patting his shoulder at the same time in warm welcome. Apparently, he didn't know about Brent's breach with Mormonism. Or, maybe it didn't matter. Brent hoped it was the latter.

"Come in," Moab said, directing Brent into a windowed office not half bad for an intern. "What's up with the ankle boot?"

"Sprained it in Italy on a little adventure."

"Hope it gets better fast. Listen, Brent, I told Dad I'd review your case and set up the deposition. He'll oversee the rest."

"Thanks. As I told you, we've got evidence of an attempted murder in a coal mine in Price, made to look like an accident." Brent handed him the manila envelope of collected notes.

Moab shook the envelope out on his desk and began to decipher the handwritten notes directly on to his laptop while Brent waited, unable to take his eyes off the evidence envelope.

"You look like you just went to a funeral," Moab said.

"I did. Otto Carr's."

"Wait, isn't he the victim here? He *died?*"

"I didn't tell you? Yes, he woke up from a coma and everyone thought he was getting better. Then he had a brain hemorrhage about a week ago."

"My condolences to your friend. This puts a new spin on the case. Now it's murder in the first degree."

"Are you sure you still want the case?" asked Brent.

"Just a sec, let me look through this evidence for a while. What's this photo?"

"I snapped it at the funeral when Ammon pointed a guy out to me as a possible perpetrator."

Moab bobbed his head. "I see," he said. He studied some of the other material for a few minutes. "Yes, we agree to represent Ammon Carr and his family," he said. "You've got a solid case built here. Good job, Brent."

"Is there a chance we can win?"

"We wouldn't take the case unless we knew we could win. Tell Ammon he won't need to appear in court unless he wants to. Meanwhile, Dad says he and the janitor need to stay out of Price for a while."

"I thought the same, and brought them here. They're downstairs. What about their families?"

"We'll make sure the families have a private guard," Moab said. "Anyway, the perps will go after you guys, because you've got evidence."

"Where should I put them up? Is there a safe house?"

"I'm between roommates for the present, so bring them to my place. You can hang out there, too, cousin."

"You're kidding, right? Your apartment in the Gateway building?"

"Yep. And we can give them a small stipend during this time. Think of it this way. It helps them *and* us because we can prep the case with them close by. As for you, Brent, Dad thinks you have some major talent for the law. He wants to hire you as an intern here at the firm so you can work on this with me."

"With only two years of college? Thanks, I need a job. We're in a money crisis at my house."

"What's going on?"

"Apparently, Dad's had some business dealings in Las Vegas and cashed in our accounts. Mom put the house up for sale. She says there's no money to pay the mortgage."

Moab looked at him, openmouthed. "Don't tell me your dad is hanging out with Uncle Ethan? Is Brother Herndon involved?"

"How'd you guess? You must know something I don't."

"We do know and my dad's going to be on it like a bee on honey. If your dad's about to get into trouble, there's strings we can pull to bring him back. We're his attorneys."

"Thanks. I knew you and Uncle Henry might have some ideas. And I know I'll love working here. I'm grateful for the job. I'll show up for work tomorrow morning."

"Tell the secretary on the way out to give you the new employee forms. Hey, I'll see you tonight. Here's my extra key. You know where the building is on State Street. There's a great sushi place down the block where we can eat."

Swooping up the key, Brent laughed, trying to picture Mike and Ammon eating sushi. "Thanks, see you later tonight."

Chapter Twenty-Three
Faithful and Just

"You guys like my cousin's place?" Brent asked, as they entered Moab's bachelor high-rise apartment in one of the trendiest shopping districts of Salt Lake City.

"Awesome," said Ammon, who'd regained color in his face. His wrinkled brow was smooth now, making him look more hopeful.

Mike's eyes were round as quarters as he looked down at the sidewalks below.

"Lots of people down there," he said. "Big city."

Brent bolted the door, and said, "Moab wants us to make ourselves at home. Tomorrow at the deposition, he's going to film you, Mike, describing what you saw."

"Okay by me," Mike said, switching on the TV. "This is an expensive sound system. Everything here looks like pictures in a magazine."

Brent pointed to a tiny inconspicuous camera in the corner. "There's more security here than a bank."

Ammon peered around. "Right. I see alarms on all the doors and windows, too."

Looking worried, Ammon said, "What about our families? My mom said some rough-looking guy rang the doorbell looking for me."

"Tell her the lawyers hired a private security guard at your house for as long as it takes. They're headed there right now. You, too, Mike. We want to make them feel safe, not threatened. Call your families and explain the armed security coming."

Each of them took their phones into separate bedrooms.

After they drifted back into the living room, Brent said, "There's one more thing. We have to record every phone call and you've got to keep all emails and texts you receive. Don't delete anything."

Mike nodded, and turned up the volume on the TV.

"I hope we can win," said Ammon, going with Brent into a bedroom to unpack.

"Moab and my uncle think you have a solid case. And Ammon, if there's a settlement you can go back to college," said Brent.

"That would be amazing," his friend said, a faraway look in his eyes.

"And then marry a woman you *really* love. You know who I mean."

Ammon looked at Brent with raised eyebrows and laughed. "First I have to ask her out," he said.

■　　■　　■

Brent pored over legal papers while Ammon organized them into piles. Mike lay on the couch, laughing at a comedy.

Ammon's phone rang, and Mike muted the TV.

"Don't recognize the number, but I'll answer. Hello?" he said, putting it on speaker.

There was a pause, then a dreadful voice echoed inside the room, slow and methodical. "You rotten scab. You're like your pa. He ain't alive no more cuz he was scum . . . never paid who he owed."

Ammon's hand shook as he adjusted the phone on the table. Brent signaled for him to not say anything, and set his own phone to record.

The creepy voice continued, "All his gamblin' got him where he is, six feet under. Old Otto got what he deserved."

Ammon shook with anger, obviously having a hard time being quiet. Brent motioned for him to pick up the phone and speak to the horrible man on the other end.

"Who is this?" Ammon asked, anger in his voice.

"My name don't matter none; I know who done the deed."

Brent slipped him a quick note.

"Are you willing to testify in court?" Ammon said, reading the note.

"Ain't going to be no court for Otto's accident." This was followed by a rasping laugh.

"You're wrong. There is going to be a trial," said Ammon, "and we'll win against whoever 'done the deed'."

"You can't prove nuthin'." The phone screen dimmed as the call ended.

Mike had listened closely to the call and began to pace around the perimeter of the room. "I'm not sure I want to be a witness," he said. "Maybe I shouldn't be here."

Brent put his hand on his shoulder. "I know all this is scary for you, but don't you think a murder should be punished? We will do our utmost to protect you the entire time, you have my word on it."

Mike took a deep breath. "I suppose I have to trust you," he said. "I can't go back to Price now."

"We'll be right here with you," said Brent, "won't we, Ammon?"

Ammon's reddened face showed the intensity of his feelings. "Thanks for stepping up and telling me what you saw, Mike. Now we have to keep going. Did you recognize the voice?"

"I think so," said Mike, "but I don't remember his name."

Ammon looked deep in thought. "This guy must know someone in the Human Resources office. That's the only place he could get my cell number. I just got it a few months ago when I got back from Argentina."

"Could mean this conspiracy runs deep," said Brent, "maybe into management. We won't be able to trust many locals or police. Let's get an App set up to record any more calls on your phone, Ammon. We're stacking the evidence here, guys. We'll find out who it was."

"I didn't know you were a lawyer," Mike said to Brent.

"I'm not, I'm just starting as an intern. I'll go to law school when this is over."

Mike grumbled under his breath. "You want to be one of those lawyers? They're all crooked."

"Hold it. My idea of lawyering is different than those greedy ones you hear about. I'm not in it for money, but for justice. There are a lot of bad people who should go to jail for what they do to good people."

"Okay . . . I see your point," said Mike. "I just hope it won't pull you into being greedy like all the rest."

"Don't worry. I'm set on being honest like my cousin, Moab. He's as truthful as they come. On that note, let's order in something to eat," said Brent, hearing his stomach growl. "You guys don't like sushi, do you?"

They both stared at him.

"How about a pizza delivery?" said Ammon. "It's almost six."

"Okay," Brent said, laughing. "When Moab gets home, he can have the sushi bar all to himself." He saw Ammon look at Mike quizzically.

Ammon ordered online just as Brent's phone buzzed again.

An unknown caller. Hot on a case, he answered fast.

The voice on the other end was a woman's. "This is Davis Hospital. Are you Brent Joseph Young?"

"Yes." Why would the hospital call?

"There's been a traffic accident. Your mother is in ICU; her status is critical. The EMTs had a hard time stabilizing your sister, they almost lost her. Can you come to the hospital right away?"

Somehow he said he would. How could this happen?

And the timing . . . Brent took a deep breath and told his friends he had to leave. Moab would cover for him.

Chapter Twenty-Four
Groanings Too Deep for Words

Alex had been waiting for Jenn to call for over an hour. His phone lit up, but he saw it was only Brent.

"What's up?" Alex asked, pressing the phone closer to his ear as he picked up the panic in Brent's voice. When the terrible news sunk in and reverberated inside his head, the world around him blurred.

He only heard Jennalee had been badly hurt. The family's new SUV had been T-boned on a left turn. She could be dying. He had to go to her.

He dove into his truck and headed for the freeway. Shifting to high gear, he sped into Davis Hospital's Emergency Room entrance twenty minutes later.

She couldn't die. Not now, not when their 'happily ever after' was so close. It wouldn't be fair of God to take her! If only he'd been with her; he might have been able to stop this from happening.

He begged the clerks at the entrance desk to allow him in to see her, but they refused. Waiting for what seemed like hours, he paced several times around the parking lot, trying to pray, until his brother-in-law-to-be screeched his brakes as he drove into the emergency driveway.

"Sorry, rush hour going north was terrible. How long have you been here?" Brent said, when Alex walked over to his car.

"I don't know, about an hour. Brent, they won't let me in because I'm not family, even though she has my ring."

"C'mon," said Brent, "You're family to me. Let's get you in there." He paused, then asked, "Hey . . . she didn't text you or anything, did she? She was really anxious to talk to you."

"No, I worried about that, too. I didn't get anything from her. She was supposed to call me when she got home so I don't think she drove distracted."

They pushed up to the desk where Alex had begged for entry over an hour before. "We're here to see Marjorie and Jennalee Young," said Brent boldly. "I'm son and brother, and this is my sister's fiancé. Wedding's planned and she's got a ring."

The receptionist gave Alex a cold stare. "You have to wait here. After Mr. Young comes out, you can go in with special permission. If any other closer family members come, you'll have to wait."

Alex grabbed Brent's arm. "Find out what's happening. I'll be here in the waiting room."

He sat down in a chair near the door and called his mom.

"I'll come and wait with you," she said.

"No, Mom. You need to sleep off your jet lag," he said. "I called because I thought you should know about this."

"Alex, it's not far. I'll be over soon."

Relief flooded the core of his being. He didn't feel too spiritual at the moment and knew his mom would support him no matter what, especially if Jenn died . . . but no, he could not even think about the possibility.

I'd give all I have, Lord, if you'd make my girl be okay. And her mom, too. Anything else would be too horrible to think about.

Why hadn't Jennalee told him about her father taking her wedding money? If he'd known this during their last conversation, he wouldn't have lost his temper, failing her once again. Didn't she realize that lack of money couldn't stop them? People got married all the time with no money.

Bitterness ate at his insides as he waited for Brent to come out. Something must be really bad for him to be inside so long. Alex knew nothing of her injuries. Would the doctors have to shave her hair off like his had been? Or way worse, would she lose a limb?

But it didn't matter what might have been done to her on the outside, or what scars she was left with, because he loved her for her entire self. She was his best friend, his gift from God. That love expanded his heart and rocked his world as he waited . . . and waited.

Alex saw the grayish piles of snow outside the window and felt dirty, too, after being on a plane for eleven hours. What a way to reunite with Jennalee. Fighting sleep, he chose a stiff couch to sit on in the waiting room. Before he knew he'd even fallen asleep, he woke when someone touched his whiskery face.

It was his mother, looking fresh. She hugged him a long while. "I prayed on the way here," she said, "and I not only hope, but firmly *believe* everything is going to turn out well."

Alex's grief erupted. "I don't know, Mom. The EMTs almost lost her. This can't happen to me again. All the people I love are taken away from me."

"Let's sit over here for a minute," said Gina, indicating a corner couch away from the other visitors.

"Mom, I failed Jenn, over and over. I'm not good enough for her. That's why things don't work out for us."

"None of us are good enough, Alex, but we can depend on a mighty God for everything we need. Right now, even in this waiting room."

She bent her head, pouring words from her soul in solid prayer, the kind of intercession that broke hearts. Alex held a deep ache in his bones that could not be spoken. A dry sob shook his shoulders.

His mother took her words down to a whisper. As he listened, the ache dissipated and a renewed trust in his Master took its place. Even if he lost the love of his life, he knew where to find strength to endure it. Peace hit him like a wave.

Under her glasses, his mom's eyes were teary, but triumphant at the same time. "With him, all things are possible. 'Remember to lean not . . .'"

"'. . . On my own understanding.' I can't anyway, because I *don't* understand."

"Alex," she said, "the Holy Spirit is doing a mighty work here. For some time, I've wanted to tell you how your father embraced my family just like his own from the very start. Yes, even with our Giovanini craziness. Now's the time to step up, son. You have an opportunity to do the same."

Jeff had said there'd be an opportunity. And his mom used the word 'embrace'. God was giving him an opportunity to embrace Jennalee's people. He needn't worry, God would give him love for them. He felt stronger.

■   ■   ■

A minute later, Brent punched open the double doors.

"Alex! Jenn's going to be okay. She finally woke up. She's got cracked ribs. The medics said she was in shock at the scene, but she's out of it now. The car's so smashed it's hard to see how anyone got out alive. They showed me a picture."

Alex looked up to the ceiling. "Thank you, Lord," he said, his mom seconding it.

Brent grinned. "Jenn is demanding they let you in. But I'm not sure they'll allow you, Mrs. Campanaro."

"It's alright. Tell us about your mother, Brent."

"Mom's critical but stable, whatever that means in ICU talk." Brent looked solemn.

"I will pray," she said. "But I've got to go home and get some sleep. Alex, I'll call later. Hug Jennalee for me." She kissed Alex's cheek and went out to her car.

Brent still had a limp gait with his ankle boot, but he walked fairly fast. He led Alex through the maze of shiny-floored hallways and up an elevator. Fixated and anxiety-ridden, he saw both their faces reflected by the glass windows under the fluorescent lights. Serious faces.

"I guess it could be a lot worse," Brent said. "And I know this sounds heartless, but I've got to get back downtown. There's nothing I can do here anyway and I shouldn't leave Ammon and Mike alone. We have an important meeting in the morning."

"It's okay," said Alex, "I'll let you know if anything happens."

"Can I ask a huge favor?" Brent said, digging in his pockets for something. "Can you spend a few nights at my house with my brothers? I have a neighbor staying there today for a few hours, but not overnight. Her name's Opal

Taylor, and if you get there before eight, she'll show you the ropes."

"Sure, I can." Alex was tired, but he could put sleep on hold.

Brent handed him a house key. "Sorry, I won't be back for . . . I don't know how long, but I'll keep you informed." He indicated a half-open door in the middle of a hallway. "Jenn's here, in Room 2048. Tell her '*Ciao*' for me."

Alex nodded, slipping the house key into his pocket. Then, straightening his shoulders, ready for anything, he strode into the dim room.

On the pillows, a pair of blue eyes shone from a puffy, bruised face. Jennalee was covered with scrapes on her neck and arms. Her torso was tightly bandaged. Two IV units made her look small in the bed, like a hurt baby bird fallen out of the nest.

"I'm here, Jenn," he said, "I waited a long time . . ."

"Alex," she cried, holding out her arms for a hug.

He pressed forward and gently placed himself in her arms, kissing her betadine-soaked hair.

"You must've prayed," she said, "because I only have three broken ribs. And they're watching a tear on my spleen. Did you hear about my mom?"

"Yes, critical but stable. That's good, Jenn."

She slowly shook her head up and down. "I shouldn't have made the turn. A huge truck came out of nowhere. It shot the red light and hit Mom's side. I don't remember much more; it's like it happened in slow motion. Alex, do you know what happened to the other driver? Were there any passengers? Are they all okay?"

"I heard a nurse say the other driver walked away from the accident. Nobody else was in the truck."

"Oh, that's good," she said, shivering. "I'm glad no one else got hurt . . . Alex, can you get me a blanket? I'm freezing."

Alex looked around. No blankets.

He walked to the nurse's station. Nobody there. Down the hall, he spied a pile of blankets in a heated glass unit and took out two cottony coverlets.

Walking back into room 2048, his heart leaped. She looked dead. Then he spotted soft breathing movement through the bandages around her ribs, and calmed himself. Covering her with the warm flannel, he pulled a chair up next to the bed.

But before he could sit down, he remembered Marjorie Young in ICU. Exhausted, he willed himself to stand up and go find her. He followed arrows to the Intensive Care Unit and disregarded a sign saying the ICU was closed to visitors. Alex went down the hall anyway, passing windowed doors until he recognized a woman on the bed in one of the rooms. Outside the door, he stretched his hand towards Marjorie Young, and began to pray for her healing in full hearing of anyone walking by.

As he prayed, fears of being the forever outsider melted and an invisible weight lifted from his spirit. Alex resolved to take his mother's wise words about his father and put them into action. He'd treat Jennalee's family like a son and a brother, not merely an in-law.

Alex swung back towards the staircase and almost ran into the back of a man in a dark suit. He excused himself, but the man was a fast walker and was already down the hall.

Back at 2048, Jennalee still slept. He added a blanket to keep her extra warm, and sneaked out. It was getting late, and he had a job to do.

Chapter Twenty-Five

A Righteous Gentile

Alex put his thumb on the ringer at Jennalee's house. Immediately, the porch light switched on and the door was opened by Boston, the second of her brothers.

"If you want Jennalee, she's not here," the teenager said. His body language wasn't unfriendly, just surprised.

"Hi, Boston. I'm here to speak with Opal Taylor. Is she here?"

Boston openly scowled. "She's in the kitchen."

Unsure if the scowl was for him or for the neighbor lady, Alex entered the foyer.

"You can wait here in the white room and I'll go get her." Boston indicated a tiny carpeted room to the right of the front door, decorated with heritage family portraits and a photograph of the Salt Lake temple. He sat down on one of the comfy chairs.

Before the teen left, Alex asked, "Why do you call this the white room?"

Boston let out a patient sigh. "You really don't know? It's because it's the cleanest room in the house for when the visiting teachers come. Or the bishop."

"Oh, I get it, like a front parlor."

"Whatever," Boston said, spinning around on his tennis shoes to go get Opal Taylor.

Alex looked at the historical picture of the temple in Salt Lake, as he prayed for courage to withstand rejection from the rest of the household. As he stood waiting in the claustrophobic room, across the foyer he spotted an enormous dried-up Christmas tree dropping needles on the expansive living room carpet. A few plastic totes surrounded it, like someone had started taking it down but was interrupted.

The sound of cartoons came from the basement stairs and Alex assumed the youngest kids were watching TV. He didn't know how much they knew about the accident and wanted to ask this Opal person.

In a few minutes, a woman slid into the room, wiping her hands on a dish towel. When he introduced himself as Jennalee's boyfriend, she greeted him coolly and listened to his question.

"The boys know only their mom and sister are in the hospital after a small car accident," Opal said, frowning and dodging Alex's eye contact. "I told them they'll be back soon. The boys are very young, and we can't traumatize them with details. Not unless the worst happens."

Alex changed the subject. "Brent Young won't make it back until day after tomorrow, so he gave me the overnight shift here for a few days. I just got off a European flight today, so you can be sure I'll get them to bed early." *Like right away.*

Her mouth became a thin line. "I'll be brief, Mr. Campanaro. You're walking into a strained situation, and even if you're serious about Jennalee, this family isn't going to welcome you with open arms." Opal paused, then continued, "Actually, they don't need your help. I've set up caregivers from the local ward. They're bringing meals in and caring for the boys, even overnight. This is our Stake President's family, mind you, and we'll take care of them."

Opal delivered quite the spiel, but Alex persisted. "I was told you have no one for tonight."

"Well, not tonight, but we're set for most of the rest of the week. Unless Brent returns, of course." She looked at a schedule on her phone. "I actually don't have anyone to pick the boys up from school, but I'll work on it."

"Let's make this simple," said Alex. "I'll be here tonight and every day and night, all week. I'll pick up the boys from school and drop them off. You won't need anyone else."

"Except you're . . . that's unnecessary. We'll manage. I'll find . . ."

"Mrs. Taylor, thanks for arranging for the boys' care so fast today, but this is my future family. And I have a key from Brent." He held up the house key. "With their father gone, Brent's the boss, isn't he?"

Opal's mouth resembled the first letter of her name. "That surprises me," she said, shaking her head. "Brent knows our ways . . ."

"He also knows me and counts me as family."

"Apparently, you can s-stay, then," she said, stammering. "However, I will pick up the children for church early on Sunday morning if you can get them ready." She looked out the window and pointed to his old truck.

With disdain in her voice, she said, "And that's a problem. You won't be able to take the boys to school in *that*. The Youngs' SUV is wrecked, but they have a Ford Fusion in the garage. The keys are by the back door."

"You're right," he conceded, "they'll be more comfortable in Jenn's car. No worries, I've driven it before."

■　■　■

When Opal left, Alex headed downstairs with apprehension to talk to the boys. He waited for the brush-off from them, but was surprised how happy they were that he was there instead of Mrs. Taylor.

"Alex, do you want to play Mario or Madden NFL?" asked Logan. "Take your pick."

"Madden, definitely," said Alex. He played a game against Boston and Logan, who were so good together, they easily beat him.

Boston warmed up towards Alex. "Okay," he said "did you let us win? Because we beat you too bad."

"I didn't let you win, I promise. I just got off a long plane ride, and I'm so tired, I can't even think. But I'm also starving. How about pizza?"

"Yes!" said Cade. "I hardly ate anything at dinner . . . Mrs. Taylor cooked it."

When the pizza delivery arrived, it was almost nine o'clock. The boys ran for their piggybanks. Alex paid the driver.

"Don't bother, guys, this is on me," Alex said. He peeked inside the box.

"Would you look at that pizza? *Delizioso!*"

They found paper plates and settled at the huge kitchen table to chow down.

"When is Mommy coming home?" Cade asked in a tired voice. "And when's Daddy getting back from Vegas? He should be here."

Yes, he should. "I don't know the answers, Cade," Alex said, "all I know is, Brent told me to be here with you guys. Which means I'm staying as long as you'll have me."

"I hate the neighbors coming over," said Jordan, glancing at his brothers.

"And nosy Mrs. Crockett across the street, asks too many questions about Dad." Logan folded his arms on the table.

Alex looked at the huge empty pizza box. It must cost a fortune to feed this family.

"I look at this way," said Boston, "if Brent sent you, you're the best pick. We'll stick with you. Tomorrow, your brother Gabe should come over to help your game."

Alex laughed and yawned at the same time. "Gabe would like that. Hey, what kind of brother-in-law am I to keep you up so late on a school night?"

"Did you two get married?" asked Boston.

Whoops. Her parents had not been told yet about their engagement. Alex hesitated, then said, "No, not yet, but I love your sister and I want to spend the rest of my life with her. Which means we're going to be. . ." He put his hands out in an inclusive motion. "Family."

No one said anything, which made Alex itch to break the silence. "You like Italian food, don't you? When I get in a cooking mood, I make a mean Alfredo."

"Alex," Jordan said, "we didn't know you before, but I think you're fun."

"You won't have to read us the Book of Mormon tonight. You can go straight to sleep," Cade said, yawning.

"Yeah," said Logan. "You let us stay up late. Will Mom and Jennalee be okay?"

"Sure, they will. Your mom has two broken legs, a cracked rib and bruising inside. Jennalee has broken ribs and they're watching for a rupture in her spleen." He pointed to his chest. "Inside here. God saved them both through a bad wreck."

"Mrs. Taylor wouldn't tell us anything and we thought they might be . . ." Logan coughed instead of saying the word. "Don't you think it's unfair to not tell us? Like we're babies or something."

"You should be told the truth. I know what it's like to have someone you love sick and hurt, and not know whether they're going to die or not." Alex winced when his tired voice cracked. "My dad had cancer."

"Did he die?" asked Cade, as Boston tried to shush him.

"He did." Alex took a deep breath as he saw each pair of blue eyes cloud with sadness. "Don't worry though, your mother and Jennalee won't die. They're in good hands."

"Mommy might. She has something else wrong. Right here." Jordan held a fist to his gut.

"God can help the doctors figure it out and heal her. Your mom will be fine. It's time for bed, so get your pajamas on and meet me in the guest room where I'll sleep. We're going to say bedtime prayers like none other!"

Chapter Twenty-Six

Love in the Fire

Alex must've slept so hard he didn't hear the sound of his alarm for several minutes. Annoyed, he finally turned it off and got his bearings. Casting his eyes on the honey-colored room in the light of dawn, he realized a miraculous God had placed him in the guest room of the house where Jennalee had grown up.

He stretched and felt warm inside, with a sense of belonging he'd never had before. Outside the window, the morning sun set alight the vertical planes of the Wasatch mountain cliffs behind the house. Winter sparrows chattered at the brick sill as he pulled on yesterday's clothes.

The boys would need breakfast and a ride to school. So *this* is what had kept Jennalee so busy the week before he flew back. Now he knew why she seemed preoccupied and hadn't communicated much. After waking the kids, he hustled downstairs to cook.

By the time breakfast ended, the sun had melted patches of ice in the streets. The boys hurried to get into the car with their backpacks and lunches. As the younger ones disappeared into their elementary school, Boston waited in silence to be driven to high school. Remembering the angst in his own ninth grade year, Alex asked how he was doing.

"It's okay, but my old friends have changed. They know about all our family stuff, which is none of their business, but . . . hey, can you bring your brother Gabe over to hang out today after school?"

"Sure." It was the second time he'd mentioned Gabe. Last year, Boston hadn't been ready to make friends with Alex's brother. He handed him his phone. "Here's his number in case you can't find him in the crowded halls."

Boston copied it into his phone and reluctantly got out of the car to go inside.

"Have a great day," said Alex. "Because it won't be so great when you get home and I beat you at Madden." The teenager's face brightened and he waved.

Glancing at the sticker in the corner of Jennalee's car windshield, he hoped the day would leave time to fit in an oil change. There was so much to do.

Alex stopped by his empty house and changed clothes. He packed more for the week, then went in search of some coffee in the kitchen.

Bless her, his mom had left a warm carafe. He got out his favorite mug and spotted an envelope with his name on it leaning against the flower vase where his mom had put Jeff's welcome bouquet.

Yawning, he slit it open and almost dropped his mug. A cashier's check fell to the counter and he saw the amount as it floated down. 50,000 Euros! It was drafted in his name and Brent Young's. He couldn't believe his eyes.

He snatched the accompanying letter. It was printed on Bernardino Vineyard stationary and relayed thanks for the return of the stolen wine. About twenty family members had signed it, along with their personal notes. Liliana's scrawled signature was there, too.

Staring at the unbelievable gift before him, strong emotions rushed back. He gulped down more coffee and called Brent and his mom, leaving them messages. His mother called back right away.

"Hi, honey. I didn't know what was inside but I told them I'd give it to you."

He told her the amount. "It's too much, Mom."

"It is indeed, but they can no doubt afford it, Alex. And now you and Jennalee are set. She'll recover, honey, I know she will. And you two will have the best wedding ever."

"Mom, first I'm paying back Uncle Lucio for the Maserati's insurance deductible. That was what finding the wine was about."

"Oh, Alex. He would want you to keep the reward money."

"To tell you the truth, Mom, I don't feel like I deserve it. I basically thought the wine was mine until Brent started asking about possible owners. I wanted to keep it myself, but I did tell him if we found a label, we'd return it. And there was *one* label out of all those bottles. One."

"Son, no matter how you came to that place in your heart, you did the right thing in the end. This has God's name attached; it's a gift to you for your faithfulness in the midst of trouble."

"I guess so, Mom. Thanks. Hey, I have to stay at the Youngs and help out. It's so busy over there, I can't go to college this semester."

"I know, *caro*. It's who you are. College will still be there when you're ready. Got to go, my class is here. Love you. *Ciao*."

Even though he was home in his mom's kitchen, suddenly, Alex felt uncomfortable. God had orchestrated his life so that suffering in a jail cell had actually *helped* him and the sheer idea of such Providence overwhelmed him. But at the same time, he was hiding sin from God. And inside the core of his being, he knew God desired more from him, way more.

He didn't want to surrender and open the door to the dark, bitter part of his heart. After all, he'd hidden only a *little* resentment and anger. Other people carried a lot more than he did. As he tried to dodge conviction, the Holy Spirit's piercing gaze zeroed in on him. He remembered the same uneasiness buzzing around his head like a bee back in the Bernardino's house. It was when he heard how *Signora* Liliana forgave the Nazis who'd murdered her father.

There was no use going on this way. He got on his knees, right there in the kitchen. "I'm sorry, Lord," he prayed. "I'm holding hatred in my heart for the Putifaros and the mafia men who imprisoned me. And I could be capable of doing even worse, except for your grace." He gulped, feeling a heavy verdict sitting on his shoulders, telling him the Holy Spirit wanted more. "And I need to forgive the people here in Utah who reject me and whisper behind my back. You know, the ones who make me feel alone. Help me forgive Jennalee's parents and their Church for not accepting me. Or not accepting you, I'm not sure which."

There was one more. "And I need help forgiving Bridger Townsend for being a big . . . stupid . . . wait, I don't mean that. Well, I do mean it, so help me forgive him, too." He raised his head. Heaviness faded as the words came out of his mouth, and gratefulness filled his heart.

He needed to see Jennalee. Shaking the painful memory of her bloodless face on the hospital bed, he prayed, "Thank you Jennalee's life didn't end yesterday and for bringing me home. Like King David said, 'Create in me a clean heart and renew a right spirit in me.' Give me love for her family and the strength to endure. Most of all, *your* will be done, not mine."

He got up, holding the check in his hand. "And wow, thank you for this, Father God."

He drove to the hospital with new resolve. Before taking the elevator to Jennalee's room, he stopped at the accounts desk. Alex planted his feet at the desk and stared at a young clerk until he got his attention. A few other people, staring curiously, milled around the waiting room.

"I'd like to pay for Jennalee and Marjorie Young's bill," he said, a little too loud in the quiet area.

"Let me see," said the clerk, punching computer keys. "We don't have an exact amount yet. You'll have to wait for everything to clear the insurance company."

"Yes, ma'am. I'll give you my email so you can send me those bills."

"Okay, Mr. Campanaro. You're a member of the family? Not that it matters *who* pays."

"I'm Jennalee Young's fiancé."

"This is a first," said the clerk.

■　■　■

When Alex got back to the Youngs' house to do dishes and take out the trash, a message blinked on their landline phone. Wondering if he should listen to it, he busied himself by tossing the first of many loads of laundry into the washer. Then, thinking it might be a message from the hospital, he pressed 'Play'.

A deep authoritative voice startled him.

"Hi, boys, this is Dad. I'll be home next Friday around dinner time. Do your homework and be good for Mrs. Taylor. See you soon."

It was the voice of Rulon Young, obviously a man used to being obeyed, announcing his arrival home . . . to take control. Alex swallowed hard. In a way, he felt relieved the showdown with Jennalee's father would happen soon. And he couldn't be more ready.

■　■　■

The evening and following week went by in a flash of taking kids to school, picking them up, cooking, and getting his job back at Starbucks. He still hadn't conquered his jetlag, yet he had to keep a steady pace. Brent must have been too busy to talk about the money because he'd only texted back a smiley face.

That day, Alex finished the enormous laundry and hung up shirts for four boys, then vacuumed the entire three floors of the house. After he picked the kids up from school, he stopped by to get Gabe. The six of them formed two teams of three and played basketball outside on the garage hoop until the sun went down.

"It's getting cold," said Jordan, as they went inside after the sun set. "Alex, do we *have* to do our homework?"

"Yes. That's what your dad said on his message. If you need help, you can ask me questions while I start dinner."

The smell of garlic cooking in oil filled the house with what Gabe said was an aroma from heaven. The boys stayed in the kitchen instead of going downstairs to watch TV.

"What are you making?" asked Logan.

"It's a surprise, but it starts with an A," Alex said.

"Sure is making me hungry," Cade said, "And Dad's going to love it."

"Dinner's in a few minutes," Alex said. "Wash your hands."

At that very moment, Rulon Young pounded on the front door and shouted, 'I'm home!' Alex and Gabe watched from the kitchen as his four sons rushed to him, chattering and hugging him like squirrels on a tree, each vying for their dad's attention.

"Opal? Are you in here?" asked Rulon, striding through the entrance into the kitchen, where Alex mixed the basil vinaigrette dressing for the salad.

"You're not Opal," he said in a loud voice. His eyes looked perplexed, then serious.

"No, sir, I'm Alex Campanaro, Mr. Young." Alex caught Rulon with full eye contact. Neither looked away.

Boston intervened. "Dad, Brent sent Alex to take care of us. He gave him his house key because he's in Salt Lake on business. And Mrs. Taylor couldn't find anyone to take care of her daughter and no one could stay overnight, so Alex did."

"You?" asked Rulon, standing with his chest out. "How do you know Brent?"

"It's a long story. We met in Italy when . . ."

"Never mind," said Rulon, breaking his eye contact with a grumpy glance at the dinner table neatly set with plates.

Alex forced himself to relax. "When Brent and I were at the hospital, he told me his dilemma about leaving the boys alone. He has a legal case downtown to work on for the next few months," he said with such a calm voice he wondered about it. "Your neighbors were unable to provide consistent care, so I came. I can stay, sir, for as long as I'm needed."

Rulon looked around at his sons. No matter how he'd wronged them, they looked back at him with adoration written on their faces.

"Tonight, Alex made his special Alfredo," said Logan, with a slight grin.

"Sit in your normal place, Daddy," Cade said. "We gave you the special red plate and you get the biggest piece of dessert, too."

Their father sat down and Alex noticed a baffled look overtake Rulon's face like a cloud shadow on the high plains.

"We'll get your suitcases upstairs, Dad," said Boston. "Did you meet my friend, Gabe? He's Alex's brother."

"Hello," said Rulon, in an odd, quiet voice. "Are you in the same grade as Bos?"

"Yes, ninth grade. Turns out, we're in the same math class this semester. You're going to love dinner. We make it a lot at our house. Boston and I did the garlic toast."

The imposing leader of the family nodded blankly, then asked, "Have you boys been up to the hospital to see your mother and sister yet?"

"No, Dad," Jordan answered.

"I'll take you tomorrow." His voice was *really* quiet now. "I've been at the hospital most of this week. I flew back right after it happened . . . and today, a week after the accident, they let your Mom out of ICU. But she won't be home for a long while. Jennalee's coming home in a week or two."

"That's good," Logan said, copying his dad's quiet voice.

"Dad," said Cade, "Alex already helped us with our homework so you can play Madden NFL with us if you're not too tired."

From under his dark brows, Rulon glared at Alex as he placed the Alfredo and salad on the table where everyone waited to eat. It looked obvious that Rulon didn't want Jennalee's non-LDS boyfriend in his house, nor did he want to eat a meal prepared by such an outsider.

"Bread! Forgot the bread," Alex said, reaching into the oven to remove the garlicky loaf, and avoiding the direct stare of Jennalee's father. "I think we're ready. Would you say the table grace, sir?"

The man looked conflicted. "I'm a bit tired," he said, "go ahead, uh . . . Alex."

Alex bowed his head, as did the boys.

"Our Father in heaven, thank you for saving the lives of our loved ones, and for giving us this time together. Bless this meal and bless each one here. Amen."

"Amen!" shouted the boys.

During the meal, Rulon started to relax. He said very little until he asked Alex, "Where'd you learn to cook like this?" He almost sounded friendly.

■　　■　　■

Alex alone got the boys up for school the next day. Rulon Young came downstairs at the end of breakfast as the boys got their backpacks ready to go to school.

"Okay, guys," their father said, "Now that I'm back, everything is going to be normal around here. Thank you . . . uh, Alex, for being here, but I can take the boys."

"Dad, Alex has to take us to school right now or we'll be late," said Boston, warily. "You're still wearing your slippers so you can't do it."

"Alex needs to stay with us, Dad." Logan dared to speak out. "You're too busy to pick us up or bring us to school or fix us breakfast and dinner, but Alex has time."

"Even when Jennalee comes home," said Cade, "we need help because she has broken ribs. And Mommy, too, with her broken legs."

Rulon looked lost in the flurry of opinions. "Right, okay. I understand you want him here until Brent gets back. Go get in Jennalee's car and Alex will be out in a minute."

"Don't forget to grab your lunches on the counter," Alex said, and the boys took their brown sacks and trooped out to the car, looking woeful.

Then Alex stood tall, shoulders back, to face Jennalee's father, and Rulon's face softened a bit. "There's something about you I don't quite understand," he said. "Why would you interrupt your life and help us?"

Alex said, "Because you need help. But also because . . . I may as well tell you that Jennalee and I are engaged to be married. We wanted to tell you together, but circumstances prevented that. For that reason, I consider your family like my own."

Rulon chewed his lip. "I suspected it might be something like that." He sat down at the table, still strewn with breakfast plates. "Listen, I saw you that first night in the hospital . . . you were praying . . . outside Marjorie's door in ICU. You don't belong to our faith, but there you were, praying for her healing like she was your mother." His bass voice cracked.

Alex nodded. "I remember . . . that God compelled me to pray for Jennalee and your wife. I believe in a God who heals."

Rulon cleared his throat. "So do we, but . . . what I want to say is . . . afterwards, I wandered those hospital halls for several days and nights, thinking about my life and the mistakes I made. That night, Marjorie's condition was bad, very bad. The doctors told me to expect her to . . . but after you came, her numbers changed so much that she's out of ICU only a week later."

Alex didn't know what to say. "Well, if God used me, I'm glad. He did it all. Sorry, but I've got to get the boys to school, sir."

"Give me another minute. I'll say it now . . . thank you. God heard you that night. There's no other explanation. Okay, you'd better go. Don't let those boys be late!" Rulon said, heading down the hall to his home office.

■   ■   ■

When Alex returned to wash the breakfast dishes, a BMW had just parked in the driveway near the garage. He noticed Brent unloading luggage and papers from his trunk. Standing nearby was a tall, good-looking man in a suit.

"Hey, Brent," Alex said as he got out. "About time you showed."

"Tired of playing Mr. Mom?" Brent said, laughing. "Did you get my text messages about why I couldn't make it back? Alex, this is my uncle, Henry Young, my dad's oldest brother."

The spiffy man stepped right up to Alex and shook his hand. "I've heard about you on the way here. Mainly, that you're engaged to our Jennalee. She's a great girl. Congratulations."

His sincerity startled Alex a bit. "Thank you," he answered. "If you're looking for Mr. Young, he was headed towards his den when I left."

Henry took a briefcase and headed for the house. "I'm going to draw the bear out of hibernation," he said.

Brent watched him leave before saying in a low voice, "Hey, your call about the check was sure a surprise. I meant to get back to you earlier. Those Bernardinos . . . what great people. I'm still in shock. I haven't told anyone just in case I'm dreaming."

Alex laughed. "I know what you mean. Sign it and I'll get you the money. It happens to be a good exchange rate today."

"Will do. Hope my dad's arrival went okay for you, Alex."

"Considering your father didn't like me that well before, everything went great." He grinned. "I'm not sure your dad knows what to do with a guy like me, but I was floored this morning when he thanked me for praying for your mom. I guess he saw me in the hospital, but I didn't see him."

"Wow, this accident woke him up. He told my uncle he came back from Las Vegas right away, hours after it happened."

"Yes . . . he said he wandered around the hospital for days, thinking about things. I guess that's why he didn't come back to the house for a while."

Brent nodded. "He thought Mom was going to die. And she's so much better, she even called me today. She said Dad apologized for taking the money. He wants to come back to the family and pay it all back."

"Well . . . I wasn't too sure what would happen when he first got here. It could've gone either way," said Alex, "but I think he's kind of accepted me now."

"Good. My uncle's here to help clean up the finances. He's looking to sell some family land holdings to pay debts. Moab told me to fire our realtor, so we don't have to sell the house, which is a huge relief."

"The boys would be lost without this house."

Brent blew out some air. "We all would be. But we live in a glass house, Alex. Rumors are flying about Dad being seen with a blonde. Uncle Henry's making inquiries, and probably yelling at Dad right now."

"Right. It might be hours before they resolve all this."

"So let's get some donuts and bring them up to Jennalee. Did you tell her about the reward money?"

"I told her yesterday. What are you doing with your half?"

"It'll see me through until Uncle Henry pays me. I'm an intern at his office now. And maybe it'll last for most of law school. You?"

"After I pay for the Maserati, I need it to . . .," Alex paused. "Well, I want to help pay medical bills for Jennalee."

"You don't have to do that, Alex!" Brent insisted. "You shouldn't have to pay because of my dad's money mess. We have good insurance."

"It's okay, I'm trying to get a couple of jobs with hours during the day when the boys are at school."

"Alex, you didn't hear me. You can't work and take care of my brothers at the same time. You need to go to college as planned. You've done enough. I'm going to see if one of my aunts can come."

"I'm staying, Brent, for as long as it takes. I love Jennalee . . . and everyone here. She's getting out in another week and she can't do much with broken ribs. You can't be here. When your mom comes home, she'll be in a wheelchair for at least three more months, plus she has something else wrong, the boys said."

"Gall stones, I found out. She's set up for surgery in a couple months."

"Oh, that's so much better than what I thought."

"Yeah, I thought cancer right away, too. That would be the worst. But my uncles will hire nursing care for Mom. You can't give up your life to keep our house running, Alex."

"Who says I can't?"

■   ■   ■

Jennalee could hardly wait to get out of the dull room with its incessant antiseptic smell. Lying in bed, watching insane shows on TV, she felt the keen loss of her active life for the last two weeks. Finally, waiting in the wheelchair for Alex to drive up and take her home, she tapped her feet with excitement. The hospital had given back her neck chain with Alex's ring and cross on it. She took it out of the plastic bag, and put the ring on her finger, and the cross once again around her neck.

Looking handsome as ever, he drove to the curb in her Ford and got out to help her into the front seat. She clutched her ribs as she got in, even though it didn't help the sharp pain that took her breath away. But at least she could walk, unlike her mother.

"You'll heal faster at home, Jenn."

"I can still help with the boys, Alex, even though you're staying another month."

"Those four are a lot to keep up with. I'll do most of it, and you can be the boss. Hey, I didn't want to talk about this while you were recuperating, but weren't you going to call and tell me something important?"

She had to laugh, which hurt her ribs. "I was hysterical when I told you we had to postpone the wedding. When I got home and realized my parents were in a terrible way, I couldn't see a way to continue with our plans, Alex. I was afraid my parents might reject you and stop us. Especially after I heard my dad took my wedding and college savings."

"You should've told me."

"I'm not going to hide anything again, I promise," she said. "I guess, to tell the truth, my worst feeling was shame, Alex. I was ashamed of my father. I didn't want you to know about his failures. Of course now you know everything. But at the time, I thought he may have done even worse . . . do you remember Uncle Ethan?"

"Yes, I met him at the anniversary party you took me to in Heber City," said Alex, wondering why she'd brought him up. "Is this something to do with your dad and polygamy?"

"Well . . . he was hanging out with Uncle Ethan a lot, he was gone all the time, and Brent and I thought . . ."

Alex kept quiet.

"Thank heavens we were wrong."

"I'll say. I really like your dad, Jenn, and now that he's back and things are good again, we're getting married first of May, no matter what. I've put a deposit on a bachelor condo near the college for March and April. You've got to see it, Jenn. It's tiny but nice. And when we get married, you can move in."

"Sounds good. I can't believe everything is happening, Alex! Listen, Dad's told me how great you were during all of this. There never was a battle between you and my dad, was there?" asked Jennalee.

"Your father and I are on good terms and everything's cool. Oh, yeah, he wanted me to give this letter to you. Your dad wrote it last night. He let me read it already."

"Okay, I'll read it out loud anyway."

"*Dearest Daughter,*

How grateful I am to Heavenly Father that you and Mom survived the accident. Because of what happened, I've done a lot of thinking about my life. I want to apologize for the times I wasn't here for you.

I had to cover up a terrible mistake that resulted in the loss of a large amount of money. I bought a casino with Uncle Ethan and Brother Herndon to make up for what I lost, but it was a bad deal all around.

The casino's owner, a woman named Sandra, initially impressed me with her business acumen, but that's as far as it went. I want you, your mother, and brothers to know that. There are false rumors about Sandra and me.

She turned out to be a crook and used her business smarts against me. I cut off my association with her, but not before she took all my money.

I'm sorry I borrowed from your accounts. I will get the money back. As my attorney, Uncle Henry's going to sue Sandra and sell some of the land our dad had in trust for us.

After I heard about the accident, I immediately took a taxi to the airport to catch the next flight back to Utah. I got to Davis Hospital that same night and saw Alex praying outside your mother's room. When I heard his compassion, I knew I'd judged him too harshly.

A day later, I was shocked to see him at the administration desk trying to pay our bills. I was in the waiting room and after he left, I cancelled his request and took sole responsibility.

I stayed in a hotel until I felt I had it together enough to come home and see the boys. When I got home, Alex was there, taking care of them as if they were his own blood brothers. He even cooks! I didn't have a problem with your engagement after that.

The main thing is, both your mom and I think this young man of yours is one in a million. He will make a fine son-in-law. We could not have asked for better. Marjorie and I will bless your upcoming marriage to Alexander Campanaro.

Love, Dad".

"Alex, they gave their blessing! Here it is, in black and white."

"I know. Isn't it great? What bothers me most is . . . how come I never noticed him at the hospital?"

Chapter Twenty-Seven

Incandescence

When Jennalee woke up the morning of her wedding, the world sparkled. The chosen day she'd wished for had come at last. It was Grandpa Young's birthday, a heritage day to remember forever. The bridal bouquet of soft pink roses on her dresser were a gift from Alex, reminding her he'd be completely hers that day.

She took a deep breath to see if her ribs hurt, as she did every morning since the accident. Today a tiny twinge of pain answered her but she knew she'd make it through the day.

An hour passed in a blur as Jennalee took care of last minute details. She made sure the flowers were ready and the cake delivered. Then she gave away the little gifts she'd bought for friends and family with her thanks and hugs.

From her wheelchair, Mom gave her a tight hug while the hired nurse ironed the mother- of-the-bride's dress. Her mother had rallied since Dad had come back to the family. Things were better and her mom looked radiant today. There was a hint of sadness behind her smile, but her mom was mostly happy.

The only thing out of the ordinary was that her father had disappeared all morning. She worried he'd be late to escort her down the aisle. Her mother said it was possible some Stake business had arisen. These things had often interrupted family celebrations before.

Jennalee studied her checklist, relieved no decorations would be needed at the fairy-tale garden at La Caille Restaurant and Vineyard, where the wedding would take place at four o'clock that afternoon.

Though French, the 'Quail' reminded her of Italy with its vineyard and lush European landscape. Holding both the ceremony and reception there was easier and gave her and Alex a day when everything *felt* perfect, whether it was or not. Was it over a year ago when they'd had dinner at La Caille on senior prom night?

How wonderful to have the wedding at a place where she'd first encountered a deep connection to Alex Campanaro, the kind of chemistry she'd never had for anyone else. The spark became a glimmer, grew into a consistent glow, and now a lively fire burned in her heart.

True to her promise as maid of honor, Rachel Christenson had arrived the day before. Jennalee knocked on the guest room door where she slept.

"Come in," said a sleepy voice.

"Good morning," said Jennalee, sliding in and sitting on the bottom of the bed. "Can you believe the day's arrived?"

"I was just getting up," said Rachel, throwing back the covers. "What a day this will be for you, Jennalee! I'm thrilled to be here."

Jennalee hugged her tightly. "Rachel, I have a job for you. I'd do it myself, but I'm overloaded. My bridal bouquet was delivered yesterday as a gift from Alex. But can you pick up the rest of the flower order?"

"Sure," said Rachel, springing up and putting on her jeans. "What are bridesmaids for, except to help out?"

Jennalee tossed her car keys on the bed. "Thanks, here's the address." She handed Rachel a slip of paper. "With the kind of opposition we've had in the past, let's pray no other obstacles come up. Sometimes I have a bad feeling."

"Okay, I pray best in the car," said Rachel. "But no worries, I'll keep my eyes open!"

Jennalee giggled. She would love to have Rachel for a 'real' sister, but that was up to Brent. And they would have a whole other story.

Rachel put on a light jacket. "I'll especially pray for your father and mother. I saw his reaction to the video last night at the rehearsal dinner."

Jennalee sighed. "Oh yes," she said, remembering Alex's family and friends' video direct from their vineyard in Italy. "It definitely showed how different Alex's family is than mine. I hope my parents can accept all of this. You never know."

"I will pray . . . that all goes exceedingly well, Jennalee. I better go get the flowers."

Jennalee fought happy tears as she hugged her mentor again. Rachel lent hopefulness to the atmosphere no matter where she went.

She refocused on the rest of her list for a while, then went back into her room where Alex's mother's bridal gown hung. Now it was hers, and she caressed the silk, remembering the cheerful video greeting from Italy. She'd been so happy they'd sent it . . . until she saw her parents' reaction.

Nonna and her new fiancé, *Signore* Tarentino, spoke in such rapid Italian that Alex had to interpret.

"They are sorry we had to wait for our wedding, but they said they waited fifty years! They wish for us to have long-lasting zeal for love like they have," he said.

Uncles and cousins waved, shouting 'Bravo!' in front of the Giovanini villa's flowing fountain where spring flowers bloomed in elegant urns. The camera showed the uncurling lime green leaves in the ancient vineyard and the tall cypresses lining the path to the villa.

Aunt Adriana blew kisses with her husband, Giuseppe, while Uncle Lucio implored Alex and Jennalee to return next summer. Massimo appeared with Firenza at his side, and saluted them with raised glasses, simply wishing '*Congratulazioni*'.

Little Fuglio's serious face emerged from the crowd and closed in on the camera. Never without a torrent of words, he said, "Alessandro, have I missed you! I want to tell you the Bonadellis are very, very nice to me. They try to look for my relatives and not find anyone . . . is okay. I like my new family. I wish you much happiness with the *Signorina*."

During the video, Jennalee noted her mother had looked fascinated, while her father appeared unmistakably troubled. When the video ended, she wasn't surprised when his booming voice overpowered the small room at the Italian restaurant that Gina had reserved for the rehearsal dinner.

"Alex, was the large house in the background *yours*?" Dad had said, "And the vineyards? Your family owns those, too?"

She remembered the churning in her stomach, and how she wondered if her dad might withdraw his blessing on them after seeing the extent of winemaking on Alex's side of the family. She'd told him earlier, but he obviously hadn't understood the breadth of it.

Alex answered bravely. "The villa and vineyard belongs to my mother's family, the Giovaninis," Alex answered. He added with a bit of pride, "The house is more than three hundred years old."

"I'm not sure I understand the connection with these people over there."

"I'm American, but my mother was born in Italy and this is her family. My father was an American. They met in Italy, at Aviano Air Force base. My dad's family can't be here. The few members left live on the east coast but sent good wishes."

Rulon Young kept silent during the exchange and Jennalee waited for his reaction or some bomb to fall, but there was none. That's why she thought her father might blow up *today*. She hoped not, but who knew?

Jennalee ran downstairs when she heard Rachel open the back door to the kitchen. Her maid of honor finished fitting the boxes of flowers into the refrigerator and poured herself some juice.

"How do the flowers look?" she asked.

"You chose the most gorgeous colors ever," said Rachel.

"Want a sandwich? I'm making one for me," Jennalee said, peeking into the flower boxes and pulling out cheese and lunchmeat at the same time.

"Sure, throw one together for me. Don't you have one more bridesmaid?"

"She's one of my LDS friends, and lives in Provo so she couldn't go to the rehearsal last night. But she'll meet us at La Caille in a couple hours."

"Oh, I see. Jennalee, look at the time," said Rachel, glancing at the clock. "You're still in your sweats! Grab the sandwiches and we'll eat upstairs. We've got to get ready."

■   ■   ■

As Rachel zipped up the bridal gown, Jennalee was pleased with how perfectly Gina's white silk wedding gown fit her.

"Thank goodness for Nonna, she tailored this dress so well."

"She knows what she's doing with a needle, doesn't she?" Rachel replied.

Holding the soft bouquet of pink roses, Jennalee slipped on her white kitten heels and felt almost ready. She took a deep breath. "Wait a minute. Where's the veil?"

"Hm. . . I don't know," Rachel said.

Together, they looked in garment bags, suitcases and closets. No veil.

"Could it still be in Italy?" Rachel asked.

"It could be," said Jennalee. "But I thought I saw it here. Now what are we going to do? How can I be a bride without a veil?"

"You don't need a veil. I have an idea. Let me get my curling iron. Be right back."

As she waited, Jennalee looked into the mirror, trying to relax her worry-lined face. Her mother said things often go wrong on wedding days. But nothing mattered that much because by tonight, she'd be married to the love of her life for the rest of her days.

It took Rachel a half hour to braid pink and white ribbons into Jennalee's blonde hair. She completed the look with soft curls in an up-do and a woven crown of matching rosebuds.

"The flower shop gave us all the extra buds," said Rachel. "You're a most gracious and beautiful bride, Jennalee. And you'll be clear and open before your husband, not hiding behind a veil."

Jennalee startled at the significance of that statement. "You're incredible, Rachel. I'm so honored to have you in my wedding! This was totally meant to be. I'm just now coming out from behind veils in my life."

It felt so right. Even if she had to walk down the aisle without her father, now she would look directly at Alex, without peering through any gauzy film. She would boldly proclaim her freedom from veils. *Any sort of veil.*

■ ■ ■

Tony Morris, Alex's friend from Youth group checked his spiked hair in the mirror of La Caille's men's room.

"I've never been a best man before," said Tony. "I'm shaking, I'm so nervous."

"How do you think *I* feel?" said Alex, laughing. "I've never been married before."

"What if I mess up and lose the rings?"

"You won't. I'm glad you agreed to be my best man considering what you thought about me and Jennalee in the beginning."

"Yeah, well, glad I could do this for you, bro. You remember what I told you last year when you started going out with her?"

"Do I ever? You told me to stay away from her."

"It's totally okay you didn't take my advice. I mean, I can see you two are really in love. But as your best man, I have to make sure you know what you're doing, Alex."

"Tony, I do. Jenn became a Christ-follower with an incredible walk with Jesus. There were times I doubted her resolve to follow him but she proved me wrong every time."

"Are you sure she'll be steady and faithful?"

"Realistically? No one can be sure, but I'm willing to take the risk. Let me ask you. Do you believe in us enough to stand up for us?"

Tony grinned. "I do. Wait a minute, that's your line."

"And I'm going to say it loud and clear," said Alex, "because I've never felt so right about anything! God led us here today. It's really kind of a miracle."

"So, you're not just marrying Jennalee because she's the prettiest girl ever?"

"There's that, but a lot more. I want to spend the rest of my life with a woman who outshines me in every way. I'm marrying far above my station in life, Tony. And I know she's God's best for me. I hope I'll be the best for her."

"I never would've believed it possible for an LDS girl to marry a guy like you, a born-again Christ-follower who's all-in."

A surge of happiness almost knocked Alex down like a wave. "Me neither, except she's been born-again and dived in all the way, too."

■　　■　　■

In all of Alex's life, he'd never been this overjoyed. Love filled his heart, not only for his bride, but for *everyone*. Today, love was a force that overtook him, making him feel as if he could forgive anyone who had wronged him.

A few tents were set up outside in a grassy area and white wooden archways delineated where the ceremony would take place. Smiling guests filled every row of chairs. He saw his mother on Gabe's arm walk up the path and sit in the front row. As he nervously popped his knuckles, sitting up front with Tony and Brent, Alex heard a rustling at the far end of the grassy aisle.

The opening song that Jennalee's mother had chosen, Pachelbel's "Canon", began to play. It was time. Taking a cue from Pastor Ron, he stood up with Brent and Tony at his side, shifting position so he could watch for his bride.

It was fun to see Brent stare longingly when the maid of honor, Rachel Christenson, appeared coming down the aisle in a wispy pink and white dress. After her, came a joyful Corinne Jones from high school Chemistry class, lightly walking up the aisle in a similar dress.

"Jennalee promised her she could be a bridesmaid back when they were both in the Missionary Training Center," Tony whispered.

"Jennalee told me. Hey, are you two . . .?"

Tony shrugged. "We lost track of each other until the rehearsal last night. We might . . . get reacquainted."

As the music intensified, Alex's whole being zeroed in on Jennalee, standing way at the other end of the grassy path with her hand touching her father's arm.

Rulon Young looked the proud father as he walked her up the aisle. Heads twisted around to see her and a dozen camera phones clicked. Behind Jennalee marched the four fresh-faced Young brothers with baskets of flowers that they set down at the feet of his mom and Jennalee's.

All guys must think their brides the most beautiful, but they were wrong. Jennalee radiated light, reminding him of the first time he'd been keenly aware of her gentle beauty. His mother's wedding dress fit her slender figure closely, and her hair was an intricate weave of ribbons and flowers and curls.

Today he would give himself and all he had to this breathtaking woman, striding up to him with her shining azure eyes, looking directly into his, certain of her choice.

Her father transferred her hand to Alex's, and they stood together, holding hands. He saw her mother, Marjorie, already in tears, her deep blues identical to Jennalee's. His own mother pressed her hands close to her face, as if trying to hold back tears. Next to her, Jeff Allred gave him an upward nod of confidence as he sat with his twins and Gabe.

Pastor Ron, who'd spent hours with the two of them, discussing marriage and theology and life, gave a simple message. He read about the veil in the Jewish temple ripping at the moment Jesus died on the cross. "Death was defeated that day because, far from being a victim," Pastor Ron said in a loud voice, "Jesus *offered* his lifeblood poured out as a final and forever sacrifice for us. We have only to repent and surrender to him as Master and Lord. In Second Corinthians 3:16 and 17, it says, 'But whenever anyone turns to the Lord, the veil is taken away.'"

Jennalee looked up sharply at those words. For the first time, he noticed she wore no veil.

Pastor Ron said, ". . . 'Now the Lord is the Spirit, and where the Spirit of the Lord is, there is freedom.' To Alex and Jennalee, I want to say that you are free as long as you remain in the Holy Spirit."

Next to his heart, Alex's hand-written vows seemed to burn in his shirt pocket. He'd started writing them way back in Nonna's kitchen in Italy. There'd been months of longing to deliver them and now the time had arrived.

After lighting a Unity candle together, he saw the signal from Pastor Ron to read his vows.

Looking into her eyes, he said, "Jennalee Eliza Young, you are the light of my life. What a God-moment when I met you! I learned to love another human being with more love than I thought possible. When you were away from me, I missed you with an ache that couldn't be fixed. What was I thinking when I thought I could live a whole year without you?"

His throat caught. He paused, then went on. "I never . . . want to be separated from you again. Being with you makes me forget hard times and remember the good. There'll be rough mountains to climb, but you're the only woman I would choose to climb them with me. I love you. It will always be you, Jennalee. From the day I met you on the stairs, it's always been you."

Jennalee kept her composure until those last words, when he saw tears gather and fall. She brushed them away. Then Pastor Ron nodded to Jennalee, and she spoke freely, not looking at a paper, but directly into his soul.

"Alexander Dante Campanaro," she began. "You were brave to become my friend and now my husband. You are such a true friend that you took a risk and shared the Word of Jesus with me and I am forever changed. I never would have imagined that my spiritual life would be completely new, and different than the religion I was born into, but because of you and your Jesus, I have light and love I never knew before. I love you as my husband and only you. Life may be hard, but with you by my side, I know we can make it through. We'll be together on earth for a time; I hope a long time. And in heaven, we'll be with Jesus, friends for eternity."

They faced Pastor Ron for the final words of the ceremony. "The bride and groom would like to say traditional marriage vows as well," he said. Then he clearly pronounced the old words. "Do you, Alexander Dante Campanaro, take Jennalee Eliza Young to be your wife? Will you love her, comfort her, and keep her, forsaking all others? Will you remain true to her as long as you both shall live?"

Alex held his head high. "I do."

"Then repeat after me," said Pastor Ron, "I, Alexander, take thee, Jennalee, to be my wife and before God and these witnesses I promise to be a faithful and true husband."

Alex repeated the words, his voice shaky because of a lump in his throat. Then he said,

"With this ring I thee wed, and all my worldly goods I thee endow. In sickness and in health, in poverty or in wealth, 'til death do us part."

Jennalee repeated them, too. Her firm 'I do!' echoed in his ears. He felt the Spirit of God lifting him, then resting around his shoulders like an electrical current.

"I now pronounce you man and wife," said their pastor.

Church bells rang out over the sound system, sounding exactly like Vespers in Italy. Alex looked at Jennalee in wonder. Beyond her, Marjorie Young beamed at him. Somehow, she'd managed to find a recording of bells in Italy.

He'd heard these bells during the earthquake, when everyone was desperate for help.

He'd heard them at Christmas, announcing Jesus' birth and joy to the world. In bad times, in good times, the bells were faithful. And he was a Campanaro, a bell-ringer. He wondered if bells pealed in heaven at this very moment, and was overcome with emotion. He knew his father would've loved Jennalee and her family, too.

Pastor Ron peered at Alex over his reading glasses. "Well?" he said. "It's time to kiss the bride, man!"

Jennalee looked up at him with a tiny smile. He lowered his head until his eyes neared hers and then he kissed her with a gentle promise kind of kiss, one full of hope and a future, while the bells continued to resound.

Chapter Twenty-Eight
So Near to Heaven

Tables were readied outside in La Caille's courtyard for the warm springtime evening reception. As wedding guests wandered the grounds, waiters brought appetizers. Alex, with Jennalee clinging to his arm, greeted their guests after the ceremony. He felt her grip tighten as her father and mother abruptly approached them.

"Jennalee, your vows . . .," Rulon said, hesitating. "They differed from any I've ever heard before. *Friends* in heaven?"

Alex felt the razor-sharpness of the question and was about to help her out when Jennalee answered, "Yes, Dad, *friends*. I've compared beliefs about marriage in heaven. Once I read Jesus' description of marriage in the Bible, I can no longer believe the LDS doctrine."

"So this idea is in the Bible, is it?" said her father, with an incredulous look.

Jennalee put her chin up. "It is."

Alex let out a sigh of relief as his effervescent mom, in an aqua dress, chose to stride up to Jennalee's parents at that moment.

"Rulon and Marjorie, we parents have the very best table, and they're catering Thyme Brined Chicken with Truffles for us. Please follow me and I'll show you. Our boys have their own table." She laughed. "And their own kid food."

Jennalee and Alex slipped away when the parents began to converse, and

184

he could see his mom and Marjorie chatting with gusto. Rulon seemed to have diverted his attention to the dinner table.

Alex patted Jennalee's hand on his arm and gazed at her.

A sad smile crossed her face. "In a way, we broke their hearts, Alex."

He gently reached for her hair. "I know."

■　■　■

At the bridal table, the couple sat close together through toasts with sparkling apple cider, the gourmet dinner, and the traditional cutting of the tiered cake. Soft Christian music played, yet no one ventured out on the stone patio to dance until the voice of Stephen Curtis Chapman started to sing "I Will Be Here".

Alex jumped up, saying, "Here it is. Our song, Jenn."

Jennalee kicked off her kitten heels and the company cheered as they took the floor.

Brent and Rachel followed, and even Tony and Corinne danced together. Rulon took his wife in her wheelchair and whirled her around slowly, with a loving gesture. Jeff and his mom swayed to the music, their heads quite close. Alex had to smile when he saw his old friend Madeline with her boyfriend, Roy Newman, out on the dance floor, too.

Daylight transformed to twilight and the restaurant's colorful stringed lights snapped on above their heads. All the trees were wired with twinkling lights, too.

"Jennalee, who are those girls?" Alex asked, indicating a few young women staring at Brent as he danced with Rachel.

"The daughters of some of my parents' friends," she said. "They've had their hopes up to marry Brent all their lives, poor things. One of them even dated him for a while."

Alex grinned. "Well . . . they're too late. Rachel's one-upped them."

She beamed, looking up at him. "Alex, this has been the best day of my life, and it's almost over."

"The best is yet to come," he said, kissing the crown of her head.

■　■　■

After a few more dances, Alex and Jennalee strolled around the room, shaking hands, greeting people, and talking with old friends. Her family was well-represented, with numerous uncles, aunts, and cousins. Missing, however, were the stricter members, who wouldn't attend any outside wedding, no matter what.

Corinne Jones almost tripped on her rose pink skirt as she ran up to them. "Back in Chemistry class, when you called me, Jennalee, and I filled you in on Alex, I never would've guessed that you two would get married! Thanks for including me as a bridesmaid, just like you said, Jennalee." She cleared her throat. "You helped me see how a mixed-religion relationship can work with strong love. I wish you both the best."

"Thanks, Corinne," said Jennalee and Alex together.

"I knew you finagled your way into that class," Alex said to Jennalee, who laughed.

Madeline Silva tapped his shoulder. "Our whole AP Chem class is here!" she said. "Hi, Corinne. You look great. Glad you're feeling better, too. Heard you were sick."

"Thanks. Yes, I had to come home from my mission. Got dengue fever. I'm a lot better now, and frankly, I was glad I could be here to attend this awesome wedding."

Corinne's face flushed when Tony invited her to dance. They walked under the lights to the patio.

Madeline faced Alex. "This is amazing; Alex, you and Jennalee agreeing on religion enough to get married. I didn't know it was possible."

"Well . . .," he said, "what you see is a miracle. It's not so much two religions, but a close relationship with Jesus for both of us. I wish everyone could discover this like we did. It's totally by God's grace, not us."

Madeline's face looked blank. "Well, anyway, I'm proud to know you both."

"Likewise," said Roy Newman by her side. He shook Alex's hand. "This is a fantastic wedding, congratulations. I hear you're both coming to Weber State next year. Hope to see you on campus."

Mom and Jeff looked relaxed at their table with Rulon and Marjorie.

Pastor Ron and his wife, Shannon, sat there, too, engaging the Youngs in conversation.

"They're getting more comfortable with each other, "said Jennalee. "Pastor Ron was true to his word. He spent a lot of time talking to my parents. Still, this morning I thought my father wouldn't show. He was gone all morning."

"Oops," said Alex. "I should've told you. I met him for breakfast at a café and we had a good talk, Jenn. Then I took him to Mom's to meet Jeff and Gabe."

Jennalee huffed a little. "So that's where he went. What did you talk about?"

"Mostly jobs. Like any good dad, he wanted to make sure I can take care of you. He and I discussed it at length."

"Did your job as a wine merchant come up?"

"It did. Your dad told me he was fairly shocked at the rehearsal when he saw our winery in Italy. He said you weren't raised in that lifestyle. But it's all going to be fine, Jenn."

"I don't see how. They'll never accept that kind of thing." She looked pensive as they approached the parent's table where they overheard the end of a conversation.

Alex's mom was talking. "Yes, the Bernardino family . . . you remember the family whose stolen wine Brent and Alex found . . . anyway, they offered to pay for the drinks at this wedding until I explained we weren't serving wine."

Marjorie bowed her head a tiny bit. "We appreciate the gesture."

"So, bless their hearts, they paid for the food. I couldn't stop them."

"We'll thank them personally," said Rulon, "if you give us their address."

"Of course," said Mom. "Oh, here come our young marrieds now."

"Isn't it great?" said Jennalee. "How generous people have been?"

All the parents agreed. Pastor Ron and Shannon got up to dance, offering their chairs to Alex and Jennalee.

As they sat down, Alex saw his new father-in-law pick up a wine list and leaf through it fast. He waved the list in the air, catching Alex with an intense look. Alex got ready for more questions.

"So, this is your area of expertise?" asked Rulon. "You know about all these wines? There must be fifty of them."

"Yes, sir. I'd have to study some, but I know most of them; where they're from and their distinct tastes. La Caille has a great list, but if I were the wine steward, I'd replace a few."

"Alexander," said Rulon, "I've been thinking about our talk this morning. I'd be a fool not to see your talent and business acumen in this direction."

Alex's mother leaned forward, listening. Marjorie did the same.

Rulon cleared his throat. "I've heard about your unusual talent as a wine-taster. Since you know this business so well, and I can see it's a big part of your life, it may still be a good opportunity for you. You know that we LDS do not drink alcohol, but that doesn't mean we can't allow a person to be free in the choice of their career."

Alex swallowed hard. "Thank you, sir, but I knew you disapproved and as I told you this morning, I'm determined to find another line of work."

He felt Jennalee squeeze his hand tight.

"Please, call me Rulon, I'm your father-in-law now," he said, with a tight smile.

"Okay, uh, Rulon. I have a habit of saying 'sir' because my father was in the military."

"I understand he was a good man."

Alex bowed his head, and looked sideways at his mother.

"We lost him to cancer a few years ago," Mom said, with a sadness in her voice. "We wish he could've been here today, but know he rejoices with us in heaven."

Jennalee's mother wiped her eyes. She'd been emotional all through the wedding, too.

Alex pounced on the moment to further an understanding with Jennalee's father. "About my dad . . . I want you to know he modeled temperance when it came to alcohol. We Campanaros don't believe in being drunk, and being a sommelier isn't about that."

"I understand more than you think I do," Rulon said.

Alex went on. "I value your approval but I think it best that I find another line of work in Utah. I mean to support Jennalee as best I can here."

Rulon paused. "I don't see how you'll accomplish a good living while you're both in college, but you're showing grit, young man, and I like your gumption." He offered his hand. "I can see you're a hard worker. You work any job you're good at, with our blessing," he said. "Right, Marjorie?"

Jennalee's eyes went wide and Marjorie nodded and stared at the centerpiece.

Alex's mom clasped her hands. "You are the most gracious people," she said.

"Yes, you are," said Alex, "I appreciate your thoughts on this, but my sense of smell hasn't come back yet and I honestly don't think I can be a sommelier again."

"Your sense of *smell?*" asked Marjorie. "I would've thought it was *taste* you are concerned with."

His mother answered, "In wine, you need a keen sense of smell more than taste. Of course, both go together. After Alex had a concussion, he lost these senses. There's no way to tell if they'll come back." Bending her head towards her son, she said, "For most jobs, though, a steward can read labels and taste. You wouldn't have to tell what regions wines are from with only your nose."

"You mean he could do that before?" Jennalee's father looked incredulous.

■   ■   ■

Alex excused himself and looked for a place he could be alone. In the men's room, he washed his face and stared in the mirror. In one day, his life had rapidly changed. He took a deep breath, and asked for wisdom from the One who gave it freely.

He felt an assurance that he'd done the right thing. The Youngs couldn't live with the shame of having a wine taster for a son-in-law, even if he was a huge success. They'd suffered enough humiliation amongst their community because their daughter had married a non-Mormon, much less a wine merchant.

No, he'd keep Italy as Italy and Utah as Utah. He could manage the separate cultures. And somehow, he'd find as good a job as his old one while he was in college.

Walking outside refreshed, but deep in thought, he glimpsed a white dress in the dim light of the front parking lot. Jennalee was talking with someone next to a car with its lights on. He sensed she may need him and headed across the blacktop. On his approach, he recognized Nicole, Jennalee's one-time best friend in high school. Nicole had married Bridger Townsend.

The driver in the car shut it off and got out. It was Bridger. Alex took Jennalee's elbow lightly and she acknowledged his touch with her hand.

Nicole, tight-lipped under the street light, tried to smile as Bridger came alongside her. "Oh, hello, Alex," she said. "We know we weren't invited, but we came to . . . congratulate you."

Bridger stood next to Nicole, rubbing the tops of his hands. "Well . . . uh, I came because I need to apologize to you, Jennalee, and you know what for. I acted extremely immature at prom and I now see things in a different way. I'm sorry."

Jennalee's eyelids fluttered in shock and Alex studied the big guy. His stance and lowered eyes imitated shame, but it was hard to tell if he was sincere.

"Well . . ." Jennalee said, looking from Nicole to Bridger. "I accept your apology, Bridger. Nicole tells me you're married, too. You deserve congratulations yourselves."

"Yes, thanks," said Nicole. "We just celebrated our three-month anniversary. Bridger's got a summer job with his father's campaign." She paused and looked at her husband adoringly. "Everyone thinks Bridger has a future in politics, too."

Alex almost let out an 'Aha'! Bridger Townsend had apologized because his future in politics would be in jeopardy if any word got out about his terrible behavior on prom night.

Jennalee deserved better, but no matter, not tonight. Alex's skepticism dissipated and was replaced by an overwhelming feeling of pity. The Holy Spirit had dealt with him about forgiving this particular person. So, with an inward struggle, Alex offered his hand, which Bridger eagerly shook.

"You're invited to join the party," Alex said, trying to sound somewhat friendly. "I'm sure you know some people here."

The Townsends locked their car and drifted into the lively reception, placing a card into the overflowing gift basket near the entrance.

The bride and groom stood outside the party for a moment, near the piled-up gifts basket.

"Do you believe it?" he said to Jennalee. "Who'd have thought *they'd* crash our wedding?"

She shrugged. "To tell the truth, Alex, I have no animosity towards them anymore."

"Well, I'm having a little trouble. You realize Bridger's an ambitious man and wanted to clean up his record, don't you?"

"I do. But I have to forgive him, even if he's not genuinely sorry. Scripture doesn't say anything about waiting until they're sorry."

Alex groaned. "I know, and I'm trying to forgive him, too, honest I am. In this case, you're right, I'm wrong." He laughed. "We've just been married a few hours and I can see how things are going to be. I'll have to say this hundreds of more times in the years to come."

Jennalee's smile proved her joy couldn't be marred by such people. Why should his be? She started walking back towards the patio where guests were dancing. He took her hand.

"This gets categorized with Romans 8:28," Jennalee said.

Alex chafed under the Spirit's conviction again. "You mean '. . . that in all things God works for the good to those who love him . . .'?"

"And 'who have been called according to his purpose.' That's exactly what I mean, and I believe it, especially tonight." She picked up the sides of her dress, her hair now escaping wildly in curls around her face. "One more dance?"

■　　■　　■

Brent and Rachel successfully slipped away from the wedding reception and the curious eyes of his family. Holding hands under the starlight, they strolled in La Caille's vineyard, pretending they were in Italy.

"You are a great dancer, Brent. No more twisted ankle either!"

"It healed pretty fast," he said. "So how do you like Utah?"

"It's just as extraordinary as Italy," said Rachel. "What a fantastic sunset we just saw, and now look at the moon and stars shining on the mountains! Isn't it beautiful?"

She held her arms close, as if she was cold, and Brent took off his suit coat and wrapped it around her shoulders. "I'm so glad you came, Rachel . . . and that you like Utah."

Rachel looked dreamily up at the Wasatch. "Spectacular, aren't they?" She gazed at him, her eyes questioning. "The culture *is* foreign, though, just like Alex told me. I must've seen about forty missionaries in suits and ties at the airport. And there's an uptight kind of feeling here. I can't put my finger on it."

"Could be the religion, it's the biggest thing here. Permeates everything," said Brent, wondering if he should ask the question preying on his mind. He went ahead. "Now that you see how it is here, do you think it's going to be easy for Alex and Jennalee, coming from such different belief systems?"

Rachel closed her eyes for a second and took a deep breath. "Think about it; they've had so much happen to them; life and death stuff. They're more mature than lots of people their age. If they listen closely to God, they won't lose their footing."

"I hate to be pessimistic," said Brent, "but Latter-day Saints believe if you leave the Church, you sacrifice being with your family in the highest heaven. It's a betrayal." He paused. "But I'm glad my parents have handled this pretty well so far."

Rachel frowned a little. "There's always a cost in following Jesus, sometimes great cost. And you have to expect those who don't know him to misunderstand."

"I know what you mean. You'd think people would rejoice with you that you're closer to God, and you see life more clearly, yet they want to pull you back down into their way of thinking."

"Right," said Rachel, "but Alex and Jennalee have begun to live genuine and honest lives, even in a society that may be against them. And they're over-the-top in love with each other."

Brent pursed his lips. "Yes, but coming from this culture, I'm not sure love is enough. Love can grow cold, with society against you. Like in *Anna Karenina*."

"My word, you are a pessimist! They're not like the characters in Tolstoy's book at all. Brent, don't you believe in love? I do. Love triumphs! And not only love, but truth. We can overcome the past if we give our 'utmost for his highest' as Oswald Chambers puts it."

Brent didn't know who Oswald was, yet liked the feisty way she said it. "What you're saying is: if we do our utmost for Jesus, there's no stopping us?"

"We absolutely cannot lose. We're more than conquerors in him," said Rachel.

Suddenly aware of more people strolling in the vineyard, Brent looked around to see if any were too close. "In Utah, you're always aware of listening ears. Talking like this can be a risk. Anyway, I'm glad my parents came through this wedding in a good way. It could've been worse. I knew it and Jennalee knew it."

Rachel squeezed his hand. "Mm-mm. Your parents are trying hard to understand and accept."

He paused as they angled back to the party. "What are your plans now that you're out of YWAM?"

"Back home to Portland. I miss my family. Then nursing school in the fall," she said.

His heart sunk. "When are you leaving?"

"In two days. You know I only came for the wedding; I have to go back and look for a summer job."

He took a slow breath. "You could stay here and look for one, Rachel. I'll help. I've been busy with Ammon's court case, but I'll take time off."

She tilted her head, thinking. "I've noticed . . . Utah has some good nursing schools."

"Are you saying this for real? Do you mean you'd come here?"

"Would you like it if I did?" Her lips wore a soft smile.

"You know I would, but you wouldn't want to go to BYU with me. It's completely LDS. Maybe University of Utah?"

She grinned. "If the Lord directed me, I'd go to BYU in a minute. But I was thinking University of Utah. Are you going to continue in the law, Brent?"

"Before I say yes, and you tell me all lawyers are crooked, I want you to know I'll be an honest lawyer, all about justice, not money."

"I would never say that. I think it's great that you want to be a lawyer. How's the case going?"

"Really good, we're set up for a jury trial in another month or so. Would you believe our witness and his family moved to Murray? They got out of Price and Mike has a better job now."

"What about Ammon?"

"He's like a fish out of water at my cousin's place. So I pushed him into getting some loans and taking classes up at the University. He's looking at engineering. I don't know which kind he'll choose, though."

They sat on a bench and Rachel leaned her head on Brent's shoulder as she said, "The wedding was one of the best ever. And I'm glad it worked out with that big guy . . . you know, your former roommate from BYU. Jennalee told me about him, and all seems forgiven."

"Yeah, Bridger was a jerk to her," Brent said. "Interesting that he apologized."

"And your mom's much better."

Brent slowly nodded. "She'll be out of a wheelchair soon. And Dad's swallowed his pride in a big way. I hope it lasts."

"No worries, Brent, trust in the One who called us. My grandma used to say God never wastes a single honest prayer nor a single honest tear, not when you're chasing after him with all you've got."

Brent looked into her eyes, deep pools reflecting his. "You realize, don't you, that my whole life changed when I met you."

A hint of joy played on her lips. "It changed even more when you met Jesus."

"That's an understatement. Once I knew the truth, I *had* to chase after him. Jesus is so much bigger than I ever thought. When we're at the U of U, we can study the Bible together. There are things that make sense to my spirit, but not to my head, you know?"

"I know, God's mysteries. We mere humans can't explain everything about him. He reveals what he wants to." She stood up and faced him. The music from the stone dance floor wafted through the vineyard.

"Hey," Rachel mused, "did you say something about being *together* at the U of U?"

"I'd transfer in a minute if you went there. And if you were in Oregon, I'd go there."

Her eyes glimmered in deep thought. "Brent, think about it. We've been together in the most exciting places. We ministered to the poor in the slums of Buenos Aires; we met up in Italy to help earthquake victims; and let's not forget racing through the streets of Naples at midnight to find a hospital. So it's kind of funny that we're going to settle down and be boring college students together."

"You and me? Boring? Never, not if we learn to tango." He jumped up and took her in his arms, in a mock dance. Laughing, she tipped her head a bit towards his. Was she inviting him to kiss her?

She moved even closer. "Why don't you kiss me?" she said, her beautiful oval face nearer than ever.

He did kiss her, and it was long and wonderful, and he knew he was in love.

Chapter Twenty-Nine
The Way of a Man with a Maid

There are three things which are too wonderful for me,
Four which I do not understand:
The way of an eagle in the sky,
The way of a serpent on a rock,
The way of a ship in the middle of the sea,
And the way of a man with a maid.
Proverbs 30:18-19 (NASB)

It was too miraculous for words. Jennalee stretched her arms in her new nightgown on the first morning of a new world, the world of married love. She glanced at her ring, the ruby surrounded by tiny diamonds, in a gold setting. Before her wedding night, she'd had no idea how it would be.

It was perfect. They had waited until their wedding night and were rewarded with purest lovemaking and countless memories, when time seemed to stop as they bonded together. She would treasure all this in her heart for the rest of her life. Nothing would ever be the same now that she was entirely, wholly loved, body and soul.

From the minute they said 'I do', they crossed over from individuals to being one in marriage, one in Christ, and one together to face the world. She was the same individual person, yet Jennalee knew she'd been transformed.

From this day forward, she was wonderfully woven together with Alex in a tapestry designed by God.

Their relationship had never been a smooth road, and she realized there would be no promises of a smoother road in their future. The biggest life challenge would be to walk day by day, step by step, breath by breath, in the power of the Lord Jesus Christ.

She opened her mother-in-law's card, and read the verse written in a loving hand:

"Trust in the Lord with all your heart. And do not lean on your own understanding. In all your ways acknowledge Him, and He will make your paths straight." Proverbs 3:5-6 (NASB)

It meant a lot to have Gina contending for them.

Downstairs in their tiny student condo, Alex busied himself with breakfast for her. She smelled bacon and yes, his beloved coffee. The deep aroma of fresh ground coffee beans was something she'd *never* experienced in her own home. She sat up fast when she heard him coming upstairs with a jiggling tray. Tomorrow *she'd* cook. She was a good cook. It was the one secret Alex hadn't yet discovered about her.

■　■　■

Alex's love for Jennalee, and his longing, too, only intensified after the wedding. The first morning, as he made their first breakfast, he remembered how he'd taken her in his arms and kissed her when he carried her over the threshold of the tiny apartment the night before. He'd lived there by himself for two long months, and now she was here, upstairs in the bed he'd bought for them. He knew those first days and weeks of lovemaking and living side by side would be the best of his life.

Falling in love was one thing, but knowing you would spend the rest of your days with the person you loved was another. To live the next fifty or more years of life alongside one another had been hard to comprehend at their young ages, but they were now entwined together by strong cords of holy love for each other and for God. They were blessed. Not everyone had love like this in their lives.

They'd become one in God's sacred design for marriage, and it brought Alex great fulfillment in his role of a husband. He found it hard to believe that they would start their life together with the goodwill of so many people, enemies and friends alike. It awed him that an Almighty God had orchestrated it all.

As a finishing touch, Alex put a spring daffodil in the little vase on Jennalee's breakfast-in-bed tray. Then he headed for the stairs, balancing the tray. At their bedroom door, he caught sight of his beautiful bride sitting up in bed, and knew he was home. Together, they'd build a home for time on this earth, and they had the promise of eternity in the presence of Jesus, because they believed in love . . . for time and eternity.

THE END

Acknowledgements

Ten years after the 1968 Belice Valley Earthquake that destroyed numerous towns in western Sicily, I participated in an archaeological excavation above the destroyed town of Poggioreale. It was a thrill to be a part of a 'dig' that found traces of the Greek Empire.

During my time in Sicily, I never forgot the people of Poggioreale and their once-beautiful destroyed village. I did a lot of wandering in that ruined town and during that time I met Jesus in an experience much like Jennalee's.

I dedicate this book to the humble people of Poggioreale, who taught me so much.

Many wonderful people have contributed to this book, the conclusion of Alex and Jennalee's story. Thank you for your kind advice, Julie Hymas, Emma Hofen, and Barbara Heagy.

My friend, Jeanie Jenks, has been with me in this series from start to finish. Thank you from the bottom of my heart for your prayer, enthusiasm, and colorful input during each step of getting these books to press. What would I have done without you?

My Oregon Christian Writers critique group is one of the best. Thank you, Julie Surface Johnson for your editing, thoughtful comments and Italian expertise based on your time in our beloved Sicily. Lindy Jacobs, thank you for asking hard, deep questions, about the motivations and emotions of my characters. Thank you, Yvonne Kays. You were instrumental in catching rabbit trails and awkward sentences, as well as plotting help. I'm grateful to

Anna Snyder for bringing out needed clarifications and for your encouragement.

A big thank you to my talented cover artist, Lynnette Bonner. I'm also extremely grateful to Jason and Marina at Polgarusstudio.com for their expertise in formatting the book.

Lastly, my patient husband, Ray, gives me freedom to write and even does dishes! I know it's not easy being married to a writer, and I love him for it.

And I'm ever grateful for the faithful readers of *A Gentile in Deseret*, and *A Saint in the Eternal City*. I hope you enjoy *For Time and Eternity*. I love you all. You waited a long time; thank you for your patience.

About the Author

ROSANNE CROFT is the author of *A Gentile in Deseret*, a Cascade Award Finalist and Book 1 in the Believe in Love Series. She continues the story in *A Saint in the Eternal City*, (Book 2, 2016), and *For Time and Eternity* (Book 3, 2018). She also co-authored a best-selling Christmas short story book, *Once Upon A Christmas*, published in 2015 by Shiloh Run Press, and *Like A Bird Wanders*, an historical novel published in 2008. In addition, she contributed to *What Would Jesus Do Today? A One-Year Devotional* for children by Helen Haidle published by Multnomah in 1998. Rosanne is a staff member of Oregon Christian Writers. She enjoys biking and hiking the magnificent scenery of Western Colorado where she lives with her husband and toy poodle. Find out more about her books at RosanneCroft.com.

Made in the USA
Lexington, KY
08 January 2019